RIDE AN ANGRY LAND

A fragile peace exists between the settlers and the Apaches in Arizona Territory in the late 1870s, but long-held hatreds fester beneath the surface. Then, without warning, an ambitious, arrogant cavalry officer leads an attack on a peaceful Apache camp and suddenly the whole frontier is like a tinder box. Only Ty Wheeler, an aging army scout, can prevent a bloodbath — but is there time before the Arizona Territory is once more ruled by the law of the gun?

Books by G. T. Dunn
in the Linford Western Library:

BAD BLOOD

G. T. DUNN

RIDE AN ANGRY LAND

Complete and Unabridged

LINFORD
Leicester

First published in Great Britain in 1997 by
Robert Hale Limited
London

First Linford Edition
published 1998
by arrangement with
Robert Hale Limited
London

British Library CIP Data

Dunn, G. T.
    Ride an angry land.—Large print ed.—
Linford western library
    1. Western stories
    2. Large type books
    I. Title
    823.9'14 [F]

    ISBN 0–7089–5377–8

Published by
F. A. Thorpe (Publishing) Ltd.
Anstey, Leicestershire

Set by Words & Graphics Ltd.
Anstey, Leicestershire
Printed and bound in Great Britain by
T. J. International Ltd., Padstow, Cornwall

This book is printed on acid-free paper

1

ARIZONA TERRITORY — 1879

Ty Wheeler wiped a dusty shirtsleeve across the screen of perspiration that had formed on his sunburnt brow. He sat astride his mount surveying the wild, broken country before him. His dusty, sweaty shirt stuck to his back in the stifling, shimmering heat

Fort Dobbs lay half-a-day's ride behind him, but many a weary mile still lay ahead of him before he reached his brother-in-law's ranch. It was his first visit for more than a year, for the army was a jealous mistress. Scouting for the 9th Cavalry left him little time for himself, even though the territory had been relatively peaceful for several years. Most of the Apaches were penned up on the various government reservations. Although a few renegades still mounted occasional raids from below the border, it wasn't like the old days. The cavalry spent more time tracking horse-thieves than dealing with troublesome Indians.

As he set off again his horse gave a nervous snort and slowed its pace. 'Easy boy,' he said softly, giving the grey a reassuring pat on the neck. 'What's got you spooked?' It was then that he spotted the buzzards circling high in the sky just ahead of him. He reached for the army issue Winchester repeater strapped alongside his saddlehorn and then eased his mount forward.

When he topped the rise ahead of him and peered down into the arid, rocky plain below, his heart skipped a beat. Halfway down the slope, some twenty yards from him, a man, or more accurately, what was left of a man, lay staked out over an ant hill, wearing only a pair of tatty longjohns. Dried blood had coagulated around a gaping wound in his upper torso. A horde of angry red ants were feasting on him with obvious gusto. Wheeler eased his mount forward at the trot, his eyes scanning the terrain for any sign of danger. Having examined the sign round about to determine the number of raiders in the war party, he proceeded to bury their unfortunate victim in a shallow grave. Having accomplished his task, Wheeler returned to his horse intent on tracking the three Apaches who had ambushed the pilgrim.

He trailed them for the rest of the day across the scorched high plains. It soon became clear that they were making for the Quaker-run reservation west of Fort Dobbs, home of Porico's band of White Mountain Apaches. By nightfall, he knew he was closing in on them, but he resisted the urge to press on, for he didn't want to run the risk of blundering into their camp in the dark. He knew better than to trust in the old wives' tale that Apaches never fought at night.

He opted for a cold camp at the base of a cliff which afforded him ample cover and a good field of fire should danger threaten. After hobbling his horse nearby and feeding him some fresh oats, he attended to the growling hunger in his own belly and then stretched out on the hard ground to try and snatch some much needed sleep. But his trigger-finger remained tightly wrapped around his Winchester ready to offer an instant response to any unwelcome visitor.

Just before dawn he came awake with a start, sensing danger. At first, he heard only the shuffling of his own horse's hooves, then he caught the almost imperceptible sound of a pebble crunching underfoot. Instantly his mount's ears pricked up. Its low, nervous snort confirmed that he was not alone. The hunter had become the hunted. While continuing to mimic sleep, he tensed every muscle in his body, ready for action.

Despite his natural precautions and a propensity to sleep lightly, he had nevertheless provided them with every opportunity to pick him off at their leisure in perfect safety from behind the cover of any one of the numerous boulders scattered about the valley floor. The fact that they chose not to do so meant that they either lacked the necessary firearms to accomplish the task or, alternatively, they wished to take him alive and make powerful medicine by subjecting him to a lingering death. But if they viewed him as easy pickings, they were in for one hell of a surprise, for Wheeler was as cunning and merciless as any Apache.

From beneath the brow of his hat his partially opened eyes constantly scanned the rugged bed of the rock-strewn valley for any sign of movement. He knew that when they rushed him he would have just a split second to react. Death lay but a heartbeat away. His throat felt dry and tight, a slight film of sweat showed on his brow. But it was good to feel a little scared, for it helped to sharpen the reflexes and focus the mind.

After what seemed like an eternity, two dark shapes suddenly materialized from behind a large rock less than twenty yards from where he lay. Before they had covered half-a-dozen paces the scout was on his feet, firing from the hip. Even as he did so, he was diving for cover behind a bush to his right. He rolled over and came up on one knee prepared to fire again. The speed and dexterity of his movement belied his stocky, six-foot frame and approaching middle age. His response had caught the Apaches unawares. The two warriors lay still upon the ground, their blood already staining the ground where they lay.

Wheeler remained motionless, his eyes darting every whichway, only too aware of the fact that another Apache remained unaccounted for. It was best to wait it out and see what he had in mind, revenge or flight.

The minutes ticked by and nothing happened. Then he heard the slightly muffled sound of a horse galloping away. Although his initial thought was that the warrior had made good his escape, he resisted the temptation to boldly rise from cover, for it could have been a ruse to draw him out. Only when he was truly satisfied that he was indeed alone did he move forward.

He flipped the nearest Apache over on to his back with the toe of his boot and grunted in surprise when he was confronted by the face of Nachos, the eldest son of Porico. The brightly coloured war paint daubed on his bronzed face was perplexing, for his people had been at peace for many years.

In his prime, Porico had been a fearsome Apache. He had blazed a bloody trail across south-west Arizona for more than a decade. For a while he had managed to bring a temporary halt to the settlement of the region. His daring deeds had rivalled those of his more illustrious contemporaries, Cochise and Geronimo. Like them, the mere mention of his name had been enough to strike fear into the hearts of the bravest of men. He had out-fought and out-thought the very best the US Cavalry had sent against him, until finally making his peace when the combined effects of war, disease and hunger threatened to bring his people to their knees.

Although they could have stubbornly prolonged the struggle, he was shrewd enough to realize the futility of it all. So he followed Cochise's example and laid aside his weapons for a life on the reservation. Since the day he had scrawled his mark on the treaty he had steadfastly kept word, even when the whites had broken theirs. A handful of young bucks had drifted away from the reservation to join Geronimo in Mexico, but those who remained walked the path of peace ekeing out an existence on government handouts and the few crops they had learnt to cultivate from the poor, arid land that was now their home. Many others would have preferred to fight, but they stayed because Porico had given his word that they would live in peace. And now the eldest son of the chief lay dead at Wheeler's feet.

The second buck was unknown to him, but that was hardly surprising, for he wore the headband of the Chiricahua. He went in search of their mounts and found them hobbled by rawhide thongs 300 yards downwind of his campsite. The other Apache had evidently lost his nerve and taken off in a hurry when the shooting started. It tended to suggest that he had been young and inexperienced. Three years of reservation life had deprived many young boys of the opportunity to perfect the traditional skills of the Apache.

He led both ponies back to his campsite where he threw the body of Nachos astride what he judged to be the better of the two mounts. The second Apache he left behind to feed the coyotes and buzzards. Having turned the other pony loose, he mounted his grey and set off towards Fort Dobbs, leading Nachos' horse by the reins.

2

All day long Wheeler suffered from the effects of the burning hot sun and the constant mist of buzzing, biting insects of all shapes and sizes that seemed intent on bleeding him dry. The conditions took a heavy toll on both man and horse. Both were caked in red dust and sodden with sweat. He was, therefore, very happy when the open compound of Fort Dobbs finally came into view as a distant grey speck on the flat, rocky, red plain late in the afternoon.

There were only a handful of people present when he entered the compound. The few troopers and civilians he encountered cast anxious glances at the body lashed across the trailing pony. They didn't need any telling that an Apache corpse spelt trouble.

Wheeler dismounted wearily in front

of the single-storey, sun-bleached stone headquarters building and tied his grey to the hitching rail. Having beaten some of the trail dust from his buckskins, he entered the building to find Sergeant Thomas O'Rourke, the duty NCO, busy doing paperwork at his desk. The happy-go-lucky Irishman grinned up at the scout and said, in a thick Donegal accent, 'Well, well, if it ain't me ol' pal Ty back from visiting his kinfolks. Didn't expect to see you again so soon.'

'Never got there,' revealed the scout. 'Had a run in with some renegade Apaches. Had to kill a couple, including Nachos, Porico's oldest.'

'Holy mother of God!' exclaimed the big redheaded Irishman.

'Now I'd better go speak to Major Grant.'

'Major Grant ain't here no more,' replied the sergeant. 'He left the post just a few hours after you did. Been recalled back East.'

'Kinda sudden weren't it?'

'You know the army, Ty.'

'So who's in charge now?' queried the scout. 'Don't tell me it's that durn fool Tisdale?'

'No,' replied O'Rourke. 'New guy, name of Major James Calvin Atkinson, and a right proper English gentleman he is too,' he sneered, making it all too obvious that he had no time for the newcomer. 'All spit and polish and routine.'

'Well, best get it done. Where is he, inside?'

'No,' replied the sergeant, 'he's already retired to his quarters.'

'Then I guess I'll just have to disturb him, won't I?'

Most of the compound was already bathed in shadow as he made his way towards the officer's quarters in the centre of the outpost. His loud, insistent rapping on the door brought a quick response. He heard heavy footsteps approaching across the wooden floor and a moment later the door creaked open. 'Yes, what do you want?' snapped

13

a harsh, irritated, English voice.

'I'm Wheeler, one of your scouts.'

'I don't deal with scouts,' replied the major, dismissively. 'Go see Captain Tisdale.'

'Climb down off your high horse, mister,' snapped Wheeler. 'You got trouble brewing.'

'Trouble! In the middle of this God-forsaken wilderness,' scoffed Atkinson, pompously.

'I've got a dead Apache in the stable, mister. I'd say that's trouble, wouldn't you?' stated the scout gruffly.

Atkinson glared at him fiercely. He wasn't accustomed to being spoken to in such a way. Who the hell did this dirty, frontier tramp think he was? Making no effort to conceal his anger he said, 'Mr Wheeler, if you have some intelligence you feel is of some minor importance, then relate it to Captain Tisdale as instructed, and if he deems it worthy of my attention we'll discuss it further in the morning. Now that will be all.' Without further ado he tried to shut the door, but Wheeler was not prepared to be dismissed in such a cavalier fashion. He stuck his foot forward to prevent the door from closing.

'Out here a man learns to survive by taking the advice of those who know the land and the people who live on it better than he does. Back in the stable yonder,' he went on, indicating with a thumb back over his shoulder, 'lies the body of Porico's eldest son, Nachos. There's no telling which way the chief'll jump when he gets the news.'

'And just how did this Nachos come to die?' queried the officer, raising his eyebrows. The scout had finally won his interest.

'I killed him, 'cause the son-of-a-bitch had a hankering to take my hair!'

'Couldn't you have merely arrested him?'

'You ever tried arresting an Apache, Major?' Atkinson glared at him and

15

then shook his head. Wheeler then gave him a blow-by-blow account of what had happened.

'We will visit Porico's camp in the morning with a full company of cavalry,' said the major, when the scout had completed his report. 'It might be necessary to teach these cowardly heathens a lesson.'

Wheeler tipped his hat back and shook his head slowly from side to side. 'Believe me, Major, that ain't such a good idea,' he contended. 'Reckon that might just be the short way to start a war. Better let me ride in alone. I know the old chief; we go back a long ways. He might kill me, but I don't figure it likely. He's an honourable man.'

'I appreciate your candour, Wheeler, but as commanding officer of this post I cannot agree to your proposal,' insisted Atkinson, irritably. 'We'll go in force. I'll also take a howitzer with us to show them that we mean business.'

'You don't know Apaches,' corrected Wheeler. 'If'n you go into their village tomorrow looking for trouble, the chances are you'll get it.'

'How will they fight? They don't have any weapons.'

Wheeler laughed and shook his head. 'Don't kid yourself, Major. If'n you think they ain't got a cache of rifles and bows stashed away, you're in for a big surprise come morning!'

'Well, if you're right, then it's as well that we are going prepared, isn't it?' insisted the major, haughtily. 'I trust you will be ready to accompany us at sunup? Or perhaps I should enlist the services of one of your colleagues?'

Wheeler took a deep breath to help contain his anger. He had met many a fool in his time, but Atkinson took the biscuit. Here was a man inexperienced in Apache ways who had the arrogance to ignore the advice of one who had spent his life fighting them. His gung-ho attitude was likely to get many a good man killed. The scout knew he had to be there in the morning to try and prevent unnecessary bloodshed.

17

'I'll be ready,' he growled. 'But I hope you'll sleep on it.' Having said his piece, he left for the sutlers store to get himself a much needed drink.

When he entered the humid, smoke-filled room he found it was teeming with troopers, local ranchers and the dregs of the territory. He ignored the curious glances and nods of recognition that came his way as he pushed his way through to the bar. 'What'll it be, Ty?' asked Jock McDonald, the jovial Scot who ran the place.

'Give me a beer,' replied the scout, leaning an elbow on the improvised bar.

'By the looks of you, I'd say you've had quite a day, laddie,' said the barman warmly, as he blew dust from a so-called clean glass and filled it with warm, frothy beer.

'You're not wrong there,' agreed Wheeler. 'You had any dealings with this new major?'

'Don't get me started,' replied McDonald. 'Most of us have had trouble with that damned Sassenach! I take it you've had a problem too?' Wheeler quickly filled him in. 'Well now,' observed the Scot when the scout had finished speaking, 'it strikes me that the major could be out to win himself a little glory. You'll just have to keep him on a tight rope.'

'Yeah,' agreed Wheeler, 'but that might be easier said than done. He seems to be one stubborn son of a bitch!'

3

It was still dark when Wheeler awoke. He stretched aching muscles and joints and rose awkwardly to his feet to light the oil lamp that hung beside his bunk. The stiffness that greeted him each morning was a consequence of too many nights sleeping rough on the trail and the wild times of his youth. He fondly remembered when his body was free of such aches and pains and his reflexes were as sharp as a cat's. Not that he was so old, forty-eight was no great age, but he was the first to admit that he had reached the stage in his life where the physical demands of his job were beginning to exact a heavy toll on his frame.

Jake Parkes, the only other scout enjoying the comfort of the adobe barracks that morning, groaned loudly and turned over to look at his companion through bleary, bloodshot eyes that betrayed a touch too much hard liquor consumed the night before. 'You heading out?' he queried, stifling a yawn.

'Yeah,' replied Wheeler.

'I have a hankering to ride with you, 'less you have any objections?'

'Fine by me,' replied Wheeler, 'as long as that jackass major don't raise no protest.'

'Why should he?'

Wheeler snorted loudly. ' 'Cause he don't know his ass from his pecker,' he quipped. 'But I'll be glad of your company,' he confessed. 'If'n we get into trouble it'll be good to have someone around that I can trust.'

Atkinson raised no objection to Parkes's presence on the expedition, but he did refuse his request to consult with the Quaker agent before setting out. With every man in C Troop equipped with fifty rounds of ammunition and a day's field rations, they left the fort just before sun-up and adopted a leisurely gait as they followed a westerly track that paralelled the Gila River. Five miles out they veered away to the south-west on a direct line for the Apache village.

Less than an hour after leaving the fort, the two scouts topped a gentle rise and gazed down upon the apparently peaceful wickiups of the White Mountain Apaches a hundred yards distant on the banks of a small tributary of the Gila. Women and children were already going about their daily chores, apparently unaware of the rapid approach of the blue-coated soldiers whom they feared 'Don't look like we's expected,' offered Parkes, stroking his beard.

'I ain't so sure,' rejoined Wheeler, scanning the village with his dark eyes. 'How many bucks d'you see?'

Parkes stood up in his stirrups to survey the village. 'Not a one,' he stated, with the merest hint of unease. Settling back into his saddle, he reached inside his shirt pocket and withdrew his tobacco pouch. He bit off a chew and then offered the pouch to Wheeler, who declined with a shake of his head. 'I don't like the look of this, no sirree.'

'Stay here and keep watch,' instructed Wheeler. 'I'll go talk to the major.' He swung his mount about and cantered back towards the approaching column.

'Trouble, Wheeler?' asked Atkinson, in his usual haughty manner, as the scout halted directly in front of him.

'Could be,' he replied. 'The village lies just over the brow of the hill. Looks peaceful enough right now, but there don't seem to be any warriors present.'

'Then let's go have a look,' said Atkinson. He swivelled in the saddle to face his adjutant, barking out his orders with the speed of a Gatling gun. 'Captain Tisdale, have the men line up abreast with sabres drawn. No bugles, no fanfare of any kind. We'll canter to the brow of the hill and then hold our position to show them that we mean business.'

'Just a gall darned minute, Major,'

snapped Wheeler, angrily. 'Do that and you'll panic 'em for sure. Then there's no tellin' what they might do!'

'I would ask you to refrain from such theatrical outbursts, Mr Wheeler,' replied the major. 'When I have need of your advice I'll ask for it, until then keep quiet.'

'The hell I will,' roared the scout. 'You'll hear me out, soldier boy.'

'Why don't you just calm down a mite, Ty,' interceded Tisdale, trying to act as peacemaker. 'I'm sure the major knows what he's doing.'

'Ain't that what they said about Custer?' snapped Wheeler irritably.

'That's quite enough, Wheeler,' growled Atkinson.

Wheeler gave an audible sigh and, making a concerted effort to keep a grip on his anger, said, 'Major, over yonder is a parcel of nothin' but old men, squaws and kids. Why not let me and Parkes ride on in and see what we can find out? If'n trouble starts, y'all can come on in.'

Atkinson gazed towards a ridge which masked the camp from view. Like any weak man who has to try to appear strong he was determined to have the last word. 'It was never my intention to charge the village without just cause,' he insisted calmly. 'But we must not appear weak or indecisive.' He swallowed hard and then nodded towards Wheeler.

'Go ahead,' he said, brusquely. 'But we'll be on the ridge, and at the first sign of trouble we'll come charging in, and we won't have time to pick and choose our targets.'

'What kept you?' asked Parkes, as his companion drew up abreast of him.

Wheeler grinned. 'Slight difference of opinion between me and the major,' he revealed. 'Now let's go have ourselves a little parley with Porico.' He reached out to grab the reins of the pack-horse which carried Nachos' body, then set off down the slope at a walk.

A dozen dirty, ragged, emaciated young children moved slowly out of their way as they entered the camp. The sullen, suspicious youngsters watched them pass through nervous, hate-filled eyes. A tall youth of about thirteen suddenly stepped out of a nearby wickiup to confront them as they neared the centre of the rancheria. He made an obscene gesture, mouthed something very uncomplimentary about their parentage and spat contemptuously in their path. But when he caught sight of the body draped over the pack-horse he lost most of his bravado. Wheeler smiled benignly as he rode on by. 'Ah reckon we's about as welcome as a bear at a picnic,' mused Parkes, taking in the sea of unfriendly faces.

'Yep, but they don't appear to be of a mind to fight, so let's not do anything to provoke 'em,' replied his companion, staring straight ahead at an old, stooped figure emerging from a wickiup, carrying a thick cedar walking stick in his right hand. 'Porico!'

'He's aged a mite since I last saw him,' observed Parkes, as they drew their mounts to a halt in front of the old chief.

'Stay put and watch our backs,' said Wheeler softly, as he dismounted.

In his prime, Porico had been an imposing figure. But Wheeler hardly recognized the withered, grey-haired figure in front of him. It hardly seemed possible that this was the same cunning leader whose innate intelligence and understanding of military tactics had enabled him to lead a guerilla campaign that had frustrated the US Army for years. The old man stared coldly into the scout's weatherbeaten face. 'I remember you. You are Killer of Enemies,' he said slowly in broken Spanish, using the name the Apaches had given to Wheeler.

The scout nodded. He knew just enough of the language to get by.

Porico's eyes moved hesitantly towards the pack-horse. As was the Apache way, he fought back the pain that was welling up in his heart. Grief was not something to display in front of a stranger. 'You have brought my son back to his people,' he said, flatly.

Wheeler nodded again and pretended not to notice that more and more Apaches were closing in on them. Enmity burned fiercely in their dark eyes, but they were unarmed and offered no real threat to him. 'He died bravely,' he said.

'No,' insisted Porico, raising his voice so that all his people could plainly hear him. 'Nachos dishonoured his people! I gave my word that we would live in peace and made my mark upon the white man's paper. Nachos broke my word.'

'There were others who rode with him,' declared Wheeler calmly, hoping that Porico would name names and make his task that much easier. 'One of them was a Chiricahua.'

Porico locked eyes with the scout, as if trying to reach right down into his very soul. 'I know of him,' he declared, with a resigned sigh. 'He was a trouble-maker.' At that precise moment the troopers appeared on the brow of the hill above the camp with the howitzer clearly visible at the front. Porico pointed a long, bony finger towards the soldiers and said, 'You bring the bluecoats to punish us when we have done no wrong.'

'No,' insisted Wheeler. 'We came to return your son and to talk. A white man was killed. Your son and two others did this. Nachos and the Chiricahua are dead. The leader of the soldiers wants the other warrior.'

'No one here killed the white man,' stated the chief, coldly. A faint smile briefly flickered across the old chief's face. 'The one you hunt has gone away. You will not find him.'

'That won't satisfy the soldiers,' persisted Wheeler, fearing they were about to reach an impasse that would inevitably lead to bloodshed.

'No more talk,' interjected an angry young voice from nearby. It was the youth who had challenged the scouts earlier. Although neither Wheeler nor

Parkes spoke Apache, they could tell from the tone of his voice that trouble was brewing. 'Our chief speaks and acts like an old woman. Kill them both.'

Porico raised a hand to still the general murmur of agreement that arose from his people. 'Saldato speaks foolishly,' he snapped. 'How will he fight? With his bare hands?'

'No,' sneered the youth defiantly. 'With this!' From beneath his shirt he whipped out a rusty, Navy Colt. Before anyone could raise a hand to stop him, he brought it to bear on the shocked figure of Jake Parkes. There came a metallic click as he hurriedly fanned back the stiff hammer and pulled the trigger. The deafening explosion which followed sent the Apaches nearest to him scattering in all directions, screaming at the tops of their voices. However, the loudest scream of all came from Soldato himself. At the very instant he pulled the trigger, he dropped the weapon, flung his hands up to his face and fell wailing and

30

kicking to the ground. Years of neglect had rusted the barrel and turned the ammunition within the cylinder bad. The Colt had literally blown up in his face when he pulled the trigger, condemning him to instant blindness and the promise of an awful, lingering death.

Parkes's life had flashed before his eyes when he saw the boy pulling the trigger. He couldn't understand why he was still alive. It took several seconds for him to appreciate what had happened. Before he could react a second deafening explosion blew apart a wickiup in the centre of the village. Several others close by immediately burst into flames. The terrified Apaches instantly scattered in all directions as burning debris rained down on them from above. Parkes yelled at the top of his voice for Wheeler to mount up and ride. But Wheeler seemed too stunned to move. Porico locked a bony hand around the scout's right wrist. 'Stop this,' he pleaded desperately, in perfect English. 'Don't let them kill my people.'

Wheeler freed himself from the old man's grip and moved towards his horse, but the skittish grey shied away from him. Before he could make another desperate grab for the reins, the horse galloped away from the noise and confusion. 'God damn it, Jake, get to that fool Atkinson and stop this senseless slaughter,' he implored.

Parkes spurred his horse towards the ridge as a second shell exploded nearby. He knew that he had to reach the major before the cavalry charged the village. But before he had cleared the wickiups on the edge of the encampment, he was engulfed by an irresistible tide of blue tunics riding hell for leather into battle. Ignoring his desperate pleas to hold up, they swept on into the village, wielding sabres over their heads, yelling like banshees, totally consumed by a lust for blood. He sat astride his mount, powerless to prevent a massacre. When he heard the killing start, he turned away and walked his horse sadly towards the stream twenty yards beyond the wickiups.

The soldiers met with only token resistance. A handful of old warriors desperately tried to stem the tide of the blue advance with the few hunting knives and old bows they possessed, while the squaws and children beat a wild, panic-inspired retreat towards the rocky terrain to the south. Sabres flashed in the bright morning sun, meting out death at every turn. The lucky ones died quickly, many were less fortunate. Dozens were left moaning, twitching and bleeding to death upon the sandy earth. Others were disembowelled or had limbs severed from their bodies as they ran screaming from the burning lodges. Some of the soldiers dismounted to pursue those foolish enough to try and hide inside the surviving wickiups. The torture and indignities they heaped upon the women were far worse than anything the so-called savages had inflicted upon white settlers in the past. The pitiful, agonized screams of the helpless victims could be heard above the cacophony of gunfire, thundering hooves and animated voices.

In the ensuing mayhem a foolish, grey-haired old man boldly stepped out in front of the onrushing soldiers to beg for an end to the senseless slaughter. He was immediately bowled over and trampled underfoot. Porico, his eyes filled with tears, spread his arms to the heavens and cried aloud to the gods asking them why they had deserted his people. He then sat upon the ground and waited for death to claim him. Wheeler pleaded with him to get away, but Porico stubbornly ignored him. Almost at once, a young trooper spotted the old chief and made a beeline for him at the gallop. Wheeler raced to intercept him. He threw himself against the attacker's horse, trying to unseat him, but he simply bounced off its flanks. As he fell to the ground his head made contact with a large rock and everything went black.

The dreadful carnage continued unabated for fifteen long minutes. None were spared. The demented troopers killed them all. Even small babies were ripped from their mothers' arms to have their heads dashed against rocks or to be lifted aloft on the points of bloody sabres. When there was no one left to kill, many of the gleeful participants wandered off in search of trophies. Some settled for discarded moccasins or other Indian artifacts, others opted for more macabre keepsakes.

The senseless, stomach-churning mutilation of the dead was an act of barbarism beyond the comprehension of sane men. Unspeakable acts were performed upon the corpses by so-called Christian men, to the accompaniment of insane laughter and happy bragging. Their vile conduct transformed the once peaceful village into a living vision of Hell.

From the far bank of the stream, Atkinson sat quietly astride his horse taking it all in like a country squire surveying his estate. Acrid black smoke hung over the camp like an early morning mist reluctant to give way to the sun, as the surviving wickiups were put to the torch. 'Sound recall,' he said casually to his trumpeter. Without waiting for a reply, he spurred his horse forward at a trot towards the smoking battlefield, intent on congratulating his troops on a job well done.

4

Wheeler stirred to the sound of a distant bugle announcing recall. He groaned loudly and sat up, rubbing the back of his aching head, disorientated and confused. When he tried to open his eyes the pain and myriad of bright lights caused him to remain still. He tried to recall where he was and what had happened to him, but could make no sense of the inane laughter and excited babble of conversation all about him. Finally, when the discomfort began to pass and the mist cleared from in front of his eyes, he lifted his head and gazed at the world about him. Instantly everything came flooding back as he stared in silent horror at the tangled heaps of bloody corpses that surrounded him.

Wheeler was no stranger to death, but the grotesque tableau of mutilated bodies scattered all about caused him to feel sick to his stomach. Almost within touching distance lay the headless torso of Porico. He didn't need telling that one of the troopers had stashed the head away in his saddlebag. He climbed slowly and gingerly to his feet, straining to maintain his balance. As he shuffled forward, he suddenly felt a supportive arm take hold of him about the shoulders. He looked up into the grim face of Jake Parkes. 'God damn that bloodthirsty butcher,' snarled Wheeler. 'Where is he?'

'Right over there,' advised his companion, pointing to an area close by where the soldiers were assembling in answer to the bugle call.

'If'n you'll give me a loan of your shoulder, I'd kinda like to have myself a little chat with the major.'

Atkinson, who had remained a peripheral figure throughout the massacre, was smiling and bowing his head in response to the general acclaim he was receiving from his happy troopers.

'Men,' he announced triumphantly, above the crackle of burning lodges and the coughing of his soldiers, 'the people of Arizona have just cause to be grateful to us for what we have done this day. We have won a great victory, and in so doing have prevented another Indian war. I am proud of you.' There was great cheering and back-slapping amongst the ranks. 'Let no one ever say that we failed to do our duty.'

'Duty?' queried Wheeler harshly, pushing his way roughly through the crowd. A sudden deathly hush descended upon the soldiers. All eyes turned to face the swaying, battered figure of Ty Wheeler. 'You talk of duty and victory, Major? Who are you kidding? Look around, tell me what you see?'

'What's the matter, Wheeler? Have yuh turned Injun lover or something?' taunted one of the troopers.

'Maybe he's just a mite pissed 'cause he ain't got no trophy to take home to his gal,' suggested another.

Parkes recognized the threat of

impending violence that flared in his friend's eyes. He placed a restraining hand on his arm. 'Take it easy, pard,' he advised. 'It ain't worth a stint in the stockade. Say your piece and let's get a-going.' Wheeler looked him in the eye, nodded almost imperceptibly and then turned back to face the strutting major.

'Go ahead, Major, tell me, what you see?' asked Wheeler, making no effort to suppress the disgust that blazed within him.

'Dead Indians who no longer pose a threat to innocent civilians,' replied the officer a mite tetchily. 'Why? Do you see something different, Scout?'

'Yeah, I do,' responded Wheeler. 'I see old men, squaws and papooses.'

Atkinson shook his head dismissively. 'When one is forced to attack an enemy in his own camp it is inevitable that some women and children will get caught up in the fighting.'

'Bullshit!' exploded the scout, no longer able to contain his pent up anger. 'You didn't need to come in shooting.'

'I think you've said enough, Wheeler,' interjected Tisdale, feeling a need to offer some tangible support to his commanding officer.

'Keep your nose out of my business, Captain,' snapped the scout. 'I'm talking to the major, not his ass-licking sidekick!'

'That's quite enough!' exclaimed the major furiously. 'You forget yourself, Scout.'

'I ain't your scout any more,' stated Wheeler. 'I just up and quit.'

'And that goes for me too,' said Parkes.

'As you wish,' agreed the major. 'The army'll manage perfectly well without you.'

'We'll swing by the post and pick up our gear first chance we get,' advised Parkes, spitting out a well-chewed chaw of dark tobacco. It landed with a dull splat not far from the major's dusty boots.

'Just one more thing, Major,' added Wheeler, as Atkinson attempted to turn his back on the scouts.

'Well?' he snapped.

'If'n you look close, Major, you'll see there ain't one buck amongst the dead. That means there's a parcel of young Apaches on the prod who are gonna be madder than a swarm of hornets. You might like to think on that a while. You might also watch your backs on the way to the fort, for they ain't likely to forget in a hurry what's been done to their women and kids.' Having said his piece, Wheeler turned his back on the major and ambled away in search of his mount with Jake Parkes at his side, leaving the somewhat subdued soldiers to ponder his parting words.

5

They rode south, away from the ravaged rancheria, skirting the sickly looking corn fields the Apaches had managed to cultivate from the thin, arid soil. When they were clear of the stench of death, Wheeler reined in and gazed back at the distant smouldering lodges. He knew it was more than a village that had died that morning, it was a people's dream. A once proud nation lay broken and scattered upon the earth. 'Makes you ashamed to be white, don't it?' said Parkes glumly.

Wheeler merely nodded. The years and the miles have a habit of changing a man and the way he thinks. There had been a time when a younger Ty Wheeler would have welcomed such a scene. He had hated the Apaches with an all-consuming passion, having buried many a good friend because of them. No other tribe could match them for cruelty.

The Apache felt that they gained great power from torturing their victims. They also believed that mutilation prevented their enemies from enacting revenge in the after-life. They were also quick learners! Many of the practices they adopted had been picked up and refined from atrocities enacted upon them by Mexicans and whites, who had pretended to befriend the Indians only to turn on them for profit or greed. Taking scalps for trophies was another habit they had picked up from the Mexicans, who had always paid a bounty to anyone turning in Indian hair, regardless of whether it came from a man, woman or child.

Wheeler had played his part in the killing during the so-called Apache wars. He had much Apache blood on his hands. But somehow, somewhere along the way, hate had turned to grudging respect and a greater understanding of the Apache way of life. Unlike other Arizonians who could never bring themselves to forgive or forget, time had healed his wounds.

Despite all he had suffered personally, he felt a certain pity for their plight. They were a defeated people, abused and victimized by a patronizing government who seemed intent on breaking every promise they had ever made to the Indians. Faceless bureaucrats in Washington had proved in a comparatively short space of time that the so-called sacred treaties were simply worthless pieces of paper. It meant that just like the mighty buffalo and the cunning red wolf that had once roamed the land without number, the once proud and noble Apaches faced extinction.

'What do you figure on doin'?' probed Parkes.

'I know we ain't getting paid for doin' army chores no more, but it won't sit too well with me if'n we simply ride away and do nothing,' replied Wheeler, looking him in the eye.

Parkes gave him a broad grin, exposing a line of rotting, tobacco-stained teeth. 'Never entered my head that we'd do any such thing,' he replied.

'I'm thinking that maybe we should split up right now,' said Wheeler. 'I'd like to find out for sure what Porico's bucks are of a mind to do. Like as not most of them will skedaddle like scared jack-rabbits to San Carlos or Camp Bowie. But a few hotheads might cause some trouble. Only way to be sure is to track them and find out.'

'And what'll I be doin' while you're risking getting your hair lifted?'

'You'll be making a sweep between here and the fort,' advised Wheeler, sitting bolt upright. 'Folks'll need to be told to keep a watch on their stock and stay close to home.'

'OK,' agreed Parkes, turning his

mount about. 'Keep a grip on your top knot, pard.'

'We'll meet up at the fort sometime tomorrow.' Parkes waved a hand in the air as he disappeared into a rising cloud of red dust. Wheeler set off to circle the village in the hope of finding fresh tracks to follow, unaware that his every move was being watched.

On a hillside not fifty yards away, two young Apaches squatted on their haunches, watching the scout from behind a clump of juniper bushes. They exchanged anxious glances but remained silent, for fear of alerting the white man to their presence. As he rode away, the elder of the pair tugged at his companion's sleeve, indicating that they should withdraw down the slope to where their horses were tethered. When they reached their mounts the younger Apache broke their silence. 'He comes to look for us, Kaso.'

'Let him come, Nayasile, my knife awaits him,' replied Kaso contemptuously.

'But what of the bluecoats?'

'They only kill squaws and children,' snarled Kaso. 'Their dust tells me they return to the fort to get drunk. They do not know that Geronimo comes.'

'But will he come?'

Kaso glared angrily at his companion. 'Were you not there when the Chiricahua told Porico he was returning?' Nayasile nodded. 'Then you know he will come with many, many warriors. Our war drums will echo from the mountains once more to strike fear into our enemies.'

'Porico said it was wrong to talk of war again, that we must put the old days behind us forever.'

'He had lost his taste for battle, he talked like an old woman,' sneered Kaso. 'You know I speak the truth.'

The boy nodded. 'But how can we fight an enemy who has the power to rain thunder down upon our villages?'

'Geronimo's power is very, very strong,' insisted his companion. 'It is said that the bullets of the whites

48

cannot hurt him. We must trust him. Our dead cry out for vengeance. He will show us the way. Come, let us return to the others and make plans. Then we will send the white scout to greet his ancestors.'

6

Kaso stood erect and proud scanning the sad faces of the Apache males gathered in the narrow, rocky draw several miles to the west of the site of the massacre. There were fifteen of warrior age, the rest were young boys and old men. Many felt bewildered, scared and confused, even if they managed to hide it. They had all been sent into the hills to hide by Porico when they had spotted the dust cloud thrown up by the approaching soldiers. The old chief had hoped that their absence from the village would prevent trouble.

Porico had feared trouble from the moment the Chiricahua had arrived three days earlier with word of Geronimo's return. The messenger had ridiculed their way of life and their bland acceptance of incarceration on the reservation. His harsh words had touched a nerve within the hearts of those who remembered the old days and the old ways, when the Apache had roamed where he pleased and had never known the meaning of the word hunger. The promise of many white scalps and unlimited booty for those who would join Geronimo when he returned from across the border proved almost irresistible to a hard core of young men. But Porico's angry voice had rung out to silence the cheering. He had warned them that the squaws would only end up singing death songs for those foolish enough to ride with Geronimo. And before the mourning was over the bluecoats would come and punish all the Apaches for the crimes of the few. His cautionary words had caused the Chiricahua to arrogantly berate him. But the insults had fallen largely on deaf ears. Only two had been moved to offer support, Nachos and Kaso. Porico had simply turned his back on his son, concealing the pain and disappointment he felt deep within. The next time he had seen his son was when the white scout returned his body.

'Our dead families cry out for vengeance,' cried Kaso, anger burning fiercely in his eyes. 'Who will ride with me to join Geronimo?' When no one moved to his side, he screamed at the top of his voice, 'Who comes?'

'If we fight, we die,' said a dispirited voice from the back of the crowd.

'We are few, but the whites are many. How can we kill them all?' asked another.

'You are not Apaches,' taunted Kaso. 'Where's your pride?' he demanded, glaring at his young friend Nayasile. Kaso's eyes demanded to know why he hadn't supported him as promised. But Nayasile no longer wished to be a warrior. He wanted to run away to one of the other Apache camps and hide, but the look of contempt on Kaso's face made him feel ashamed. In spite of an inner voice counselling him to remain where he was, he suddenly found himself standing at his friend's shoulder. Kaso gave a smug grin and said, 'Who else comes?'

'I ride with Kaso,' replied a young warrior, stepping forward. 'Better to die fighting than to live off handouts like a tame animal.'

'It matters not if I die,' cried another young voice. 'They killed my family.' He pushed his way to Kaso's side.

'What about you, Chato?' asked Kaso, staring into the frightened eyes of Porico's youngest son. The twelve year old dropped his head to avoid having to look him in the eye. Part of him wanted to take up the challenge, even though he feared death. He certainly hated the whites enough to don the paint of a warrior, and he knew that in the old days many boys not much older than he had claimed scalps. But knowing of his father's wish for peace he was worried that he might dishonour his memory if he chose to ride with Kaso.

'He's just a boy,' said Guyan, an old

friend of Porico's. 'Leave him alone.'

'He's old enough to kill,' stated Kaso. 'Does he not want vengeance?' The boy lifted his head briefly to glare at Kaso, but quickly averted his eyes. 'Or perhaps he is a coward?'

'I am not afraid,' stated Chato, his head snapping up. 'But my father said we should live in peace.'

'Your father is dead, killed by the whites he trusted. You no longer have to answer to him. You're free to ride as a warrior or to slink away like a tame Apache. Make up your mind.'

Three others, two of whom were still in their teens, quickly moved soundlessly to Kaso's side. One of them was Niache, Chato's cousin. Like Nayasile before him, Chato suddenly felt compelled to join the renegades.

Kaso was a trifle disappointed to find himself leading just a handful of youths. However, he accepted the situation, confident that Geronimo would welcome any new, well-armed followers. Nayasile and Chato were the only recruits who came without rifles or bows. 'We have need of more weapons,' he announced sternly. 'You will give up your guns and bullets.'

'I will not give you my rifle,' replied Guyan, tersely. 'I need it to hunt.'

'Our need is greater, old man,' insisted Kaso.

Guyan instantly brought his rifle to bear on his challenger's midriff. 'You'll have to take it,' he said defiantly. 'If you think you can!'

Kaso's eyes narrowed, but he remained outwardly calm and composed. 'There has been enough Apache blood spilt this day,' he said. 'Keep your gun, old man. We will take what we need from the whites when we kill them.'

'I think you will all die soon,' stated Guyan, turning his back on the renegades to address the others. 'I go to San Carlos, who comes with me?' They all grunted in unison.

As the main body of Apaches moved silently away, Kaso uttered a series of urgent, staccato commands to his followers. 'Get your horses. Collect water bags. Check your rifles. Delshay, Chato, to you goes the honour of our first kill. A white scout comes. Catch up to us when you have claimed his scalp.'

Delshay looked genuinely excited at being chosen. Chato was less enthused. 'I have only my knife,' he said, dropping his hand to his side to illustrate the point.

Kaso smiled, pulled an army issue revolver from his waistband and lobbed it gently into the nervous boy's cupped hands. 'That will give you strength,' he stated. 'The son of Porico is about to become a warrior.' Then he spoke to Delshay. 'There are many hiding places amongst the rocks,' he said. 'Choose your spot well, for the scout is no fool.'

'We will not fail,' promised Delshay boldly.

Kaso nodded his satisfaction, then moved swiftly away to find his horse.

'Don't be afraid, little one,' said

Delshay. 'Killing the scout will be easy.'

'Maybe,' replied Chato, with a frown.

'I will wait in those rocks,' said Delshay, pointing to a steep escarpment off to his right. 'You stay here behind the boulders. Then we will have him in a crossfire.' When Chato nodded, Delshay slipped nimbly away to take up station high above the trail.

The metallic sound of his horse's hooves striking bare rock echoed eerily off the steep, sandstone walls of the dry gorge as Wheeler tracked the Apaches who had left the village prior to massacre. As he carefully negotiated the broken terrain, he kept one eye on the unshod tracks left behind in the sandy pockets of the draw and another on the rocky bluffs that seemed to be pressing in upon him from all sides. The prickly feeling at the back of his neck had already convinced him that he was being watched. When his grey gave a low snort he knew he was riding into an ambush. As surreptitiously as possible his eyes quickly darted left and right, high and low, trying to locate the Apaches who were lying in wait to claim his hair.

The brutally hot sun beat down unmercifully upon his back as he rode on ever deeper into the draw. The humid air felt still and stale. There wasn't even the merest hint of a cooling breeze to offset the stifling heat reflecting back off the shiny, rocky surface. Suddenly, he saw a telltale flash of sunlight reflecting off a gun barrel high up in the rocks thirty yards ahead of him. Almost immediately came the loud report of a rifle-shot and a thin puff of smoke.

He had been half anticipating the shot and was on the move a split second before Delshay's finger tightened around the trigger. He dived for cover behind a large boulder at the side of the trail, taking his Winchester with him. The Apache's shot went wide of its mark, pinging off the rocks behind the scout, sending a loose chipping high into the air. A second shot clipped the top of his hat, causing him to duck down even lower.

Having squeezed off two more shots in rapid succession to keep his quarry pinned down, Delshay rose from cover and bounded towards the rocks a few feet to his right. Before he got halfway across the narrow opening, he heard the bark of a Winchester and felt a searing pain in his chest. The force of the bullet knocked him over the edge of the cliff to land in a lifeless heap at the bottom of the gorge.

Wheeler remained alert, certain that at least one more Apache was lurking close by. For the best part of ten minutes he didn't move a muscle. Then, just when he had all but convinced himself that the Apache had acted alone, he heard his horse whinny. The animal's nervous disposition told him all he needed to know. He took a deep breath, checked his rifle to ensure that he was ready, and sat down with his back up against the boulder, conserving his energy.

He didn't have long to wait. The almost imperceptible sound of a soft deer-hide boot scraping across a loose pebble at ground level would have meant nothing to a greenhorn traveller, but to a man like Wheeler it spelt danger. He held his breath and automatically tightened his index finger around the trigger of his Winchester.

The trouble with Apaches, as many white men had found out to their cost, was that they had a tendency to defy logic and do the most unexpected things. Young Chato was no exception. Although he was in fear of his life, he was too proud and stubborn to simply run away.

Stepping on the loose pebble had been an act of pure carelessness, a mistake no battle-hardened Apache would have made. But the boy was inexperienced in stalking an enemy. Such things were no longer taught on the reservation, for it was no longer thought necessary for a boy to learn the old skills associated with manhood. He paused by a large rock, knowing that he had betrayed his presence, unsure of what to do for the best. His first thought was to risk a full frontal assault, but then he saw the scout's grey horse on the far side of the narrow ravine and a broad grin formed on his gaunt, young face. He knew he could reach it unseen. Once astride the horse he could charge the scout, firing his pistol from beneath the animal's neck. The plan might have worked had the grey not caught his scent. The horse snorted loudly and started to back away as the boy set off on a low-running, zig-zagging dash across the open ground. When he made a desperate grab for the trailing reins, the grey shied away and then reared up on its hind legs.

Wheeler sprang from cover, rifle at the ready. But when his eyes fell on the young bronzed face, his finger hesitated on the trigger. He was so surprised to find that his adversary was just a young kid that he actually ignored his basic instinct and started to lower the Winchester. It was a mistake which nearly cost him his life. The terrified boy, seeing the scout emerge from cover over his shoulder, abandoned his attempt to grab the horse's reins and swung around to bring his pistol to bear on his enemy. His hurried shot hit the scout in the side.

The last thing Wheeler had expected was for the boy to turn and fire at him. He had mistakenly reached the conclusion that the Apache was trying to steal his horse in order to get away. The sudden burning sensation in his side stirred him into somewhat belated action. 'Drop the gun,' he roared, first in English and then in Spanish, hoping the spooked youngster would understand him.

Chato was too frightened and confused to take in the strange, rapid words. He was already fanning back the hammer for a second shot as Wheeler shouted at him. The scout was forced to defend himself. With no time to aim properly, he fired from the hip. The boy cried out in pain and dropped his pistol as the force of the bullet sent him somersaulting away backwards. He landed in a crumpled, moaning heap a few feet away from the prancing horse.

Wheeler gingerly probed the wound in his side. When he brought his hand up he saw that it was covered with blood. 'God damned kid almost did for me,' he grumbled under his breath, as he ambled over to check on his attacker.

The boy's eyes flickered open when he sensed the scout's presence towering over him. He gritted his teeth against the intense pain that racked his upper body, snarled something unintelligible in Apache and then spat defiantly in the scout's direction. 'Don't figure you like me much, boy,' said the scout, with a broad grin. 'Can't for the life of me think why!'

He knelt down at the boy's side and

made to examine the wound in his right shoulder. No sooner was he down on one knee than Chato made a grab for the hunting knife he carried in his belt. But the loss of blood and pain from his wound made his movements clumsy and laboured. Wheeler managed to get a firm grip on his left wrist before the knife could do any damage. He quickly forced him to drop the blade and then kicked it away out of his reach.

'Kill me, white man. An Apache is not afraid to face death,' sneered the boy, as he fell back limply, all the fight knocked out of him. Wheeler sensed the meaning in the boy's words.

'What's your name?' he asked slowly, in Spanish. The boy averted his eyes and refused to answer, so he tried again. 'You *sabe* Spanish, my young cayuse? Eh?' He gently shook the boy's good arm to gain his attention. Chato glared up at him and grunted, trying to mask his pain from the scout.

'I am called Chato,' announced the boy.

'Porico's youngest?'

The boy gave a curt nod. 'And you are Killer of Enemies,' he sneered. Wheeler nodded. 'I came this close to taking your scalp,' boasted the youngster, raising a thumb and index finger a quarter of an inch apart. 'Now I will die bravely as an Apache should.'

'I ain't gonna kill you,' replied Wheeler. 'Now hold still while I take a looksee.' Chato held his breath and lay still while the scout examined his damaged shoulder. 'Bullet's still in there,' he announced very matter-of-factly. 'It'll have to come out or likely as not you'll end up with gangrene or lead poisoning. You need proper doctoring. I need to get you to one of the settlements.'

For the first time genuine fear flared in the boy's dark eyes. 'I no go,' he stated firmly. 'Only torture and death awaits an Apache in a white village. Better you kill me now. Take my knife, slit throat, be quick.'

'There's no need to be afeard,'

insisted the scout. 'I won't let no harm come to you, you have my word on it. Now let me patch up that shoulder as best I can and we'll be on our way.'

7

At the far end of the draw, where the land fell gradually away to form a broad expanse of undulating, rocky plain dotted with mesquite, cactus and yuccas, Wheeler reined in, dismounted and examined the sign left behind by the fleeing Apaches. The tracks indicated that the warriors had split up into two groups and headed off in different directions. The larger party, numbering about twenty, had turned east to skirt around the barren, rocky outcrop. He guessed, correctly, that they were heading for the comparative safety of San Carlos. The remainder had chosen to ride due west towards the Mexican border.

He stood there a moment, silently pondering his various alternatives. He was torn between getting medical attention for himself and the boy and trailing one or other of the Apache bands. As it appeared that both groups were more intent on flight than causing any trouble, he opted to ride for his sister's ranch in order to get aid for the boy and himself. He climbed slowly back into the saddle, wincing at the burning pain in his side, and led the way down the long slope on to the hot, dusty, inhospitable, arid wasteland which stretched all the way to the far horizon.

The intense, energy-sapping heat and tricky, undulating country made for slow going. They took regular breaks to rest the horses and drink tepid water from the scout's canteen. Each time they stopped, Wheeler made a point of checking the boy's shoulder. The Apache always steadfastly refused to show any sign of pain, but Wheeler could tell he was suffering a great deal from the effects of the bone jarring ride.

They were just two miles from their objective, when Chato's indomitable spirit and strength finally gave out. Weak from loss of blood and delirious with fever, the boy suddenly toppled sideways out of the saddle to land with a dull thump on the ground. Wheeler was at his side in a flash, canteen in hand. When he failed to revive him, he cursed under his breath. Having collected the boy's pony and tied its reins to the tail of his own mount, he carefully lifted the boy into the saddle and clambered up behind him with a painful grunt. Holding the boy firmly with his left hand, he set the grey into motion, fearing that his determined efforts to save him might end in failure.

An excited little girl's voice echoed out from the wooden porch as he approached the small, single-storey stone house. 'It's Uncle Ty!' By the time he reined in she had been joined by her surprised parents and elder brother.

The smile that initially greeted the news of his brother-in-law's unexpected visit vanished in a trice when Tod Gates's eyes fell on the limp bundle in front of the scout. 'What'd you bring that thing here for?' he demanded, tetchily. 'I don't want no stinkin' Apache on my property.'

'He'll die for sure if'n he don't rest up,' advised Wheeler, sinking back down into his saddle, disappointed but not entirely surprised by his brother-in-law's reaction. Tod Gates had lost his entire family to an Apache raid the same year that he had married Wheeler's kid sister, Nancy. Such experiences were never forgotten. 'I know how you feel about Apaches, Tod, but he's just a hurt kid for God's sake!' pleaded the scout, hoping that his brother-in-law would see sense. The two men had always been close. They hadn't exchanged an angry word in all the years they'd known each other. But the presence of the wounded Apache boy threatened to drive a wedge between them. It was then that his sister took a hand in proceedings.

'Now lookee here, Tod,' she said, stepping forward to confront her shocked husband. 'No one can say you ain't got good reason for feeling the way you do about Apaches, but it ain't right to take your hate out on a poor helpless boy. Why, he ain't no older than our Johnny.'

'Hush up, woman,' snapped the rancher, irritably, 'this ain't your concern.'

'I will not hush up!' she exclaimed angrily. 'You may be the man of the house, but that don't mean you're always right. How can you even think of letting this boy die? Please, Tod,' she pleaded, desperately. 'Don't do this dreadful thing, it'd truly be a sin. Didn't our Lord say 'suffer little children to come unto me'?'

'I don't reckon he meant no Apache brats!' exclaimed the rancher, shaking his head forlornly, knowing full well he was being out-manoeuvred. 'But have it your own way. Put the stinkin' little heathen in the house. But if'n he turns

71

on you in the night and scalps y'all, don't say I didn't warn you!'

'I'm glad it's all settled,' said Wheeler, happily. 'Now if'n you folks wouldn't mind I'd kinda like to get this little bub to bed. My arms are just about played out. I don't suppose you're of a mind to give me a hand down, Tod?'

'You brung him, you get 'im inside,' returned Gates, turning on his heels to stomp off towards the barn for a sulky smoke.

Nancy moved to her brother's side and took hold of the bridle of his horse while he dismounted, keeping a supportive hand on the boy. As soon as his feet touched the ground he winced with pain and dropped his left hand to his aching side. 'You're hurt, Ty!'

' 'T'aint nothin',' he assured her, with a forced grin. 'Just a little ole flesh wound. I'll take care of it once we've got the kid settled.'

Johnny ran to the door and held it open for his uncle and ma. Naturally, he stepped in front of his kid sister as she was about to enter! He quickly scurried after the adults, totally oblivious to the peeved hand-on-hips pose or the angry scowl that came his way.

'Put him in Johnny's bed,' instructed Nancy, pointing to a curtained-off section of the main room by the far wall. 'Johnny, you'll double up with your sister for now, you hear?'

'Yeah, Ma,' returned the freckled-faced kid, not put out in the least by the loss of his bed. That was entirely due to the fact that he intended to make his pesky sister sleep on the dirt floor!

Nancy pulled back the plain, patched curtain that screened the simple home-made bed from the rest of the room and stepped aside to let her brother lay the boy down gently on the soft, straw-filled mattress. 'He don't look so good,' she said sadly. 'I hope he doesn't die.'

'There's every chance he will, 'less I can get him some proper doctoring right quick.'

'We'd best send for old Sam Hawkins,' she said.

'The horse doctor!' exclaimed Wheeler.

'He's all there is, Ty,' she advised. 'Besides, he's patched many a bullet hole and delivered a fair few babies in his time, including mine!'

'Well, if'n he's all there is, I guess he'll have to do,' agreed Ty. 'Just keep the kid warm and comfortable, I'll be back directly.'

'You can't go, Ty,' she said, putting a restraining hand on his arm as he started towards the door. 'At least not until you get your own wound attended to and a few hours' sleep.'

'No time for that, the boy could die,' he insisted.

'Let me go,' offered Johnny enthusiastically, moving swiftly to his uncle's side. 'I can get to the settlement and back by sundown, no sweat.'

'No,' said Wheeler, emphatically. 'I'd best go myself. Hawkins will need a parcel of persuading to practise his doctoring on an Apache.'

74

'Are you sure that's the real reason?' he asked softly.

'Cross my heart,' insisted Wheeler, with exaggerated sincerity. 'I know what a good rider you are; heck who was it helped to learn you when you was hardly outa your crib?'

'You,' acknowledged the youngster, with a hesitant grin. 'Though you and Pa didn't try too hard to catch me when I kept falling off!'

'That's how you learn, bub, by fallin' off and getting right back on again,' joked his uncle, knowing the crisis had passed. 'Now I've got to get a-going.'

'Not before I dress your wound,' insisted Nancy, firmly.

Tod Gates was leaning against the end of the log barn, smoking a stogie, when his son and brother-in-law emerged from the house. He paid them no heed as they strode towards him, his son having to take two rapid steps to each one of his uncle's in order to keep pace beside him. Johnny, sensing that his pa was still sore, gave him a sheepish grin and a wide berth as he hurried on by without breaking his stride. Wheeler felt obliged to try and mend fences. 'First time I can remember us having a serious difference of opinion about anything,' he said, pausing directly in front of the stone-faced rancher. 'It don't sit too well with me, Tod.'

Gates looked Wheeler straight in the eye. 'Nor me,' he admitted. 'But a man can't help his feelings and I just can't stomach Apaches, you know that.'

Wheeler nodded. 'I knew you wouldn't be happy,' he admitted. 'And I'd never have brung him if'n he coulda made it to the settlement.'

Gates nodded and gave a low grunt. 'You going for Hawkins?'

'Yeah,' replied Wheeler, pleased that Gates had made it plain in his own way that things were right between them.

'Take my sorrel,' he offered. 'Your grey's about played out.'

'Johnny's already saddling her up,' replied Wheeler, with a wry grin. 'He kinda offered her on your behalf back in the house.'

'Then you'd best be riding,' he said, as his son emerged from the barn leading the magnificent young horse that was his pride and joy.

'I'll take good care of her,' promised Wheeler, hauling himself wearily into the saddle.

'What'll you do if'n Hawkins won't come?'

'He'll come,' insisted the scout. 'Even if I have to hogtie him to a saddle!'

8

The sun had started to dip behind the hills by the time Wheeler reached Medicine Bow. It wasn't much of a place to speak of: a few shabby timber-framed houses; a stable; a stage and freight office; an adobe-walled trading-post-cum-general store-cum-bar, all crowded together close to the banks of the stream which gave the settlement its name; and a rather incongruous white stone, spanish-style church, which stood in majestic seclusion beside a grove of cottonwood trees a hundred yards to the south. The pace of life was slow and easy. Even the numerous buckaroos from the local ranches who frequented the bar come pay day, never raised much of a ruckus. The only time the settlement drew a real crowd was on a Sunday morning, when people from miles around came to worship in the church.

For as far as the eye could see in any direction the scorched land was bathed in a glorious, breathtaking, orange glow. Everything seemed to be in perfect harmony. But he was in no mood to admire it as his mount eagerly forded the shallow stream and trotted on towards the settlement. Apart from a mangy-looking mongrel, stretched out with its head on its paws, fast asleep by the steps of the stagecoach office, the place seemed devoid of life. The dog opened its eyes as he passed by and gave a low growl. But when it sensed that he offered no threat, it lowered its head and went back to sleep.

He halted in front of the dilapidated trading-post and slipped somewhat stiffly out of the saddle, taking care to protect his injured side. Sven Carlson, the rotund, balding, bearded, jovial Swede who owned the establishment was lighting a coal-oil lamp in response to the fading light when he entered.

Three other men were seated around a battered circular table by the far wall drinking whiskey and playing poker. None of the card players paid him any heed. 'By Jiminy, Ty Wheeler!' exclaimed Carlson excitedly, in a heavy accented voice. He immediately put the lamp down on the counter and set off across the floor to greet the new arrival. 'Vot are you doing in these parts?'

'Got me a hurt kid,' replied Wheeler, nodding casually at one of the men seated at the table. 'I have need of your services, Hawkins,' he continued, turning his head to address the man facing him at the table.

Sam Hawkins emitted an exasperated sigh. 'Can't it wait, Ty? These cards are being good to me for once,' he drawled tetchily.

'No it can't,' insisted Wheeler, moving purposefully towards the table. 'The boy'll probably die if'n you don't get the slug out of him purty quick.'

'Just my luck,' complained the vet, throwing his cards down petulantly. 'Sorry, *compadres*, but it appears that duty calls.' He rose from his seat, straightened his gammy knee, a legacy from the Civil War, and walked around the table to join Wheeler. 'Where is he?'

'Out at Tod's place.'

'I'll go fetch my bag. Meet me out front directly.'

'I'll be right with you,' said Wheeler, as Hawkins disappeared through the door, Wheeler turned on his heels and strode back to the counter. 'Give me two of those penny candies,' he said, pointing to a large glass jar that resided on the shelf directly behind the anxious-looking Swede.

The trader deftly removed two of the hard, thin, red and white striped candy sticks from the jar and handed them to Wheeler. 'My treat,' he said, as Wheeler made to pay him. 'Old Sam will soon fix young Johnny up,' promised Svenson, in kindly fashion.

'He's as good with people as he is with horses.'

'Let's just hope you're right,' replied Wheeler, not bothering to correct the man's understandable misconception about the identity of the injured party. 'Thanks for the candy,' he added over his shoulder, as he took his leave.

It was almost full dark when they arrived at the ranch. A calico, quarter-moon cast a ghostly glow upon the range and a multitude of tiny, shimmering stars twinkled and danced their way across the inkyblue heavens. Gates came to meet them, lamp in hand, drawn by the sound of their approaching horses. 'How is he doing?' asked Wheeler, as he dismounted.

'Not good,' replied Gates.

'Then I'd best get to it,' suggested Hawkins, unhooking the battered black medical bag from his saddlehorn. Gates turned and led the way into the house. When the vet caught sight of young Johnny sitting at the kitchen table in his long nightshirt his eyes widened in amazement. 'What'n tarnation's goin' on here?' he demanded. 'I thought he was hurt bad?'

'Johnny ain't your patient, Sam,' advised Wheeler, with a mischievous glint in his eye.

'He is,' said Gates, pointing to the cot at the far end of the room.

Hawkins' jaw dropped a mile when he set eyes on his patient. 'But that's a God-damned Apache!' he roared in disbelief. 'I ain't tending him!'

'The hell you're not,' corrected Wheeler, firmly. 'What d'you reckon I brung you for?'

Hawkins shook his head and glared defiantly at Wheeler. 'No way,' he insisted.

'Sam, we weren't none too thrilled when my brother first brought the Apache boy here,' said Nancy, gliding across the floor towards him. 'But he's just that, a boy. And he's hurt. Can't you find it in your good Christian heart to take a look at him?'

When he looked into her appealing eyes he knew he couldn't refuse her. With a resigned sigh he took off his jacket and dropped it over a chair. 'I don't take kindly to being tricked, Wheeler,' he snapped, moving towards the wounded boy.

'Coffee, Ty?' asked Gates, as the vet went to work on his patient. 'Got a fresh pot on the stove.'

'Why not?' agreed his brother-in-law. 'I could sure use some.'

'Can one of you bring me over a lamp?' asked Hawkins, from across the room. 'I need more light to work by.' Young Johnny beat them all to the punch. He jumped up from his seat, picked up the small lamp from the table in front of him and hurried over to aid the vet, sticking his tongue out at his sister as he went past, just for good measure. Wheeler took a sip of his strong, steaming-hot black coffee and then strolled over to watch Hawkins at work. Gates went with him. The scout rested his hands gently on Johnny's shoulders as he peered down at the restless figure of Chato. His nephew turned his head to smile up at him. 'Will you keep that darned lamp still, boy?' demanded Hawkins, irritably. 'I can't see what I'm about.'

'Sorry,' replied an embarrassed Johnny, quickly swinging his head back to face him.

Five minutes later, Hawkins withdrew his stainless steel probe from the boy's shoulder and gleefully held the bullet up for all to see. Having discarded it with a metallic clink into a small enamel bowl on the floor, he cleaned the wound with sulphur powder before deftly closing the gaping hole with three neat sutures. Nancy then helped him to wrap a bandage tightly around the boy's shoulder and upper chest to protect Hawkins's handiwork. 'That'll hold him,' he advised, slowly rising to his feet. 'Keep bathing his forehead and try to get some broth into him if'n you can.'

'I'll do that,' replied Nancy, with a

warm smile. 'Will he pull through?'

Hawkins rubbed his chin thoughtfully. 'He's burnin' up with fever, and that's always a worry. You'll have to keep a close watch on him. The next twelve hours will be critical. But I reckon he'll make it. These stinkin' little heathens are as tough as nails.' He straightened his stiff knee and limped across to the room to rinse his hands and medical instruments in the bucket of fresh water which was waiting for him on the floor by the stove. After drying his hands on a rag provided by Johnny, he helped himself to a cup of coffee before taking a seat at the table next to a very quiet and bleary-eyed Lucy.

'Purty neat work for a horse doctor!' remarked Wheeler, cordially.

'So tell us about it?' replied Hawkins, coolly ignoring the observation.

The scout nodded, then walked over to the stove, poured himself another cup of coffee and sat down on the other side of Lucy. He then related his tale, leaving nothing out. 'Still can't figure out why the boy and the other young buck stayed behind to bush-whack me,' he said, when he had finished his account of the grisly events.

'What did the boy hisself have to say?' asked Hawkins.

'He weren't too communicative after I shot him!'

'What'll the army do?' asked Gates.

'Never mind the army,' interrupted Hawkins, 'what'll the other Apache tribes do when they get wind of what's happened?'

'I doubt they'll do anything,' stated Wheeler. 'The Apaches are a dispirited, broken people. They've had their day, and they knows it. Oh, sure, the news'll spook 'em some. A few hotheads might even slip away from the reservation to join up with Geronimo below the border, but we ain't lookin' at any full-scale uprising.'

'You sure about that?' pressed Hawkins.

Wheeler nodded firmly. 'I'm sure,' he

insisted. 'You ever visited San Carlos or Camp Bowie?'

Hawkins shook his head. 'Of course not,' he replied, irritably.

'Well I have and it ain't a purty sight. The Apaches are half-starved and dressed in rags. The government is trying to turn 'em into farmers, but the land ain't fit for growin' diddly squat. It's barren and dry, and the Apache ain't no farmer any ways.'

'He's a murderin', thieving savage is what he is,' insisted Hawkins, with a scowl.

'Yeah, he might be that too,' agreed Wheeler. 'It'd be kinda hard to argue the point, remembering all the things they've done in the past. But it still makes me sad to see how we treat 'em now. If something ain't done, the chances are that purty soon the only Indians left in this country will be the wooden ones outside of the town stores.'

'And what about them ol' devils Geronimo and Victorio?' asked Hawkins.

'Ain't they still on the prod?'

'Geronimo! Victorio!' mocked Wheeler, shaking his head in disbelief. 'That dog don't hunt! Sure, they jumped the reservation. But the way I figure it, they're lying low somewheres in the Sierra Madres, dodging the Mexican Army.'

'So they ain't a threat?'

'I didn't say that,' corrected Wheeler. 'Geronimo's a stubborn, bitter, wily ole fox who just don't know when he's licked. Victorio's the same. Their defiance acts like a beacon of hope for all the Chiricahuas and that certainly makes 'em dangerous. But I'll bet they'll think twice about coming back. Now, if'n you'll excuse me, I'll be turning in. It's been a long day.' With that, he rose from the table, patted little Lucy on the head and made for the door.

'Johnny, make up an extra pallet for Sam in the barn next to Ty,' instructed Gates, as his brother-in-law disappeared outside into the sticky night air. 'It's late, you'll stay over 'til moming, Sam, I won't take no for an answer.'

'I'm obliged to you,' replied Hawkins. 'And sayin' no never entered my head.'

9

Wheeler awoke just as the dawn began to spread its paintbrush on the plains. He gave Hawkins a none-too-gentle kick in the rump to get him moving. When the horse doctor raised his sleepy head Wheeler said, 'Sun's up. If'n I know Sis, there'll be bacon and grits and coffee a-plenty on the stove.'

'I'm gettin' too old for sleepin' on hard floors,' observed Hawkins, mirroring the scout's earlier stiff and laboured efforts in rising from his pallet.

The two men were still washing at the trough when Nancy appeared at the front door of the house carrying a towel. Right beside her was young Johnny, looking all bright eyed and bushy tailed. When his ma handed him the towel he promptly took it over to his uncle. 'Breakfast is on the stove,' she offered, smiling warmly.

Wheeler grinned smugly at his companion as he accepted the towel from Johnny. 'How's our patient doin'?' he asked, looking up at his sister.

'He's still burning up with fever,' she replied, making no effort to shield her concern.

'I'll take a look at him before we eat,' said Hawkins.

He found Chato bathed in sweat, turning restlessly in the bed, ranting deliriously in his own strange, harsh-sounding language. 'He don't look so good,' observed Wheeler.

'Neither would you if'n you'd travelled twenty miles or more with a bullet in your shoulder,' quipped Hawkins. He unwrapped the bandage from around the boy's shoulder and gave a satisfied grunt when he beheld his handiwork of the night before. 'The infection's under control,' he said. 'If'n we can break the fever, he'll make out just fine.'

Conversation during the meal was kept to a bare minimum as the menfolk made short work of the food on offer. 'Are you heading straight back to Medicine Bow?' asked Gates, cradling his empty tin cup in his hands as he waited for Nancy to fetch the coffee pot.

Hawkins shook his head. 'Naw,' he replied. 'Now that I'm out here, I figured I'd look in on my brother and his family. They run the relay station fer the stage company over at Apache Wells. He didn't come into the settlement for our weekly game of poker last night. I'd best make sure everything's OK.'

'If'n you don't mind the company, I reckon I might just ride with you,' said Wheeler.

Hawkins and Gates both shot him anxious glances. 'You don't figure there's a chance it could have something to do with those White Mountain bucks?' asked Hawkins.

'Doubtful,' replied Wheeler. 'But I'd like to know for sure before I lit out.'

'Suit yourself,' said Hawkins, feeling

that the scout was holding something back.

When they had finished breakfast the two men saddled their horses for the ride to the isolated relay station. 'Stay close to home today,' Wheeler told his brother-in-law, as he climbed into the saddle. 'Probably nothing wrong, but keep your eyes peeled and a gun handy, just to be on the safe side,' he added in response to his brother-in-law's puzzled expression.

Gates nodded slowly. 'I'll do that,' he agreed. 'What'll we do with the boy if'n he should wake before you get back?'

Wheeler grinned. 'Just don't spook him,' he replied. 'And brush up on your Spanish; he don't speak no English and I know you sure as hell don't speak no Apach'!'

A little over two hours after setting out from the ranch they caught sight of the relay station nestling in the mouth of a narrow gap between towering, rugged mountains. The stage company had used the pass as a short cut between Yuma and Tucson since the early 1860s. When Cochise had made his peace with Oliver Otis Howard, the old one-armed Christian general, an overnight relay station had been built at the western end of the pass, close to the fresh water springs. Jesse Hawkins had been given the job of building and then managing the place. It provided him with a home and a pretty good income for his growing young family. The work wasn't exactly back-breaking either. All he had to do was make sure he had a fresh team of horses ready and waiting for the weekly eastbound and westbound stages. His wife Martha helped out by cooking meals for the passengers.

When they were about a quarter of a mile from the adobe-walled station, Wheeler reined in. Using a hand to shield his eyes from the fierce glare of the sun, he peered at the buildings and corral through the shimmering heat. 'We got trouble,' he stated flatly.

Without elaborating further, he sank back into his saddle and led the way forward at an easy lope.

The Apaches had made short work of the station. Nothing remained of the buildings but smouldering ruins. A number of semi-naked, misshapen bodies lay scattered around the charred stagecoach. 'God damned savages!' cried Hawkins, as his eyes misted over with tears.

Wheeler drew his mount to a halt by the burnt-out stagecoach. He shook his head sadly, emitted a low sigh and dismounted. There were three male bodies lying between the barn and the blackened shell of the house. The Apaches had stripped, scalped and mutilated their victims. Some of their clothing lay scattered about the yard, but the Indians had evidently taken the men's boots and shirts for their own use, for they were all missing.

Wheeler caught his breath when he stumbled upon a figure lying amongst the ashes of the barn. He could tell that the poor young woman had endured unspeakable suffering before death had finally claimed her. Behind him, he heard the telltale sound of Hawkins being physically sick. He strolled slowly to his side and helped him back to his feet. Hawkins looked up at the charred figure hanging by his feet from a high rail over the corral gate and shook his head in disbelief. 'I hope to God he was dead when they did that to him,' he muttered.

Wheeler looked at the body and then down at the ashes of the fire the Apaches had built beneath his head and said, 'They wouldn't have bothered with the fire if'n he was already dead.'

'Damn your eyes, Wheeler, I should a killed that stinkin' Apache brat you brung in!' The scout didn't respond, for he could understand the hate that was welling up inside the man.

'Stay here,' instructed the scout. 'I'll see what else I can find.' Without giving his companion any opportunity to argue the point, he strode off towards the ruined house. When he passed by the stagecoach he swung his right boot against one of the remaining rear wheels. His disgruntled assault caused the vehicle to topple over and disintegrate with a loud, resounding crash. It threw up a choking curtain of dust and ashes high into the air.

It didn't take him long to find the bodies of the relay station manager and his wife. They were lying inside the house. The Apaches hadn't touched the woman's body, which was a sure sign that she had been killed by her own husband. The Apaches were a highly superstitious people who refused to go anywhere near a suicide. But they had mutilated the man's body, which proved they had got to him before he could turn his gun on himself.

'Did you find the kids?' asked Hawkins, when the scout returned.

'They had kids?' queried Wheeler, sounding genuinely surprised.

'Yeah. Two, Tommy, he's nine and

Sue-Ellen who just turned six last month.'

'Looks like the Apaches took them. Most likely aiming to sell them in Mexico. White kids can fetch a mighty good price on certain haciendas below the border.'

'Then we have to go find 'em and get 'em back!'

'The Apaches who did this are probably headin' fer Medicine Bow. Our first priority is to help the folks at the settlement. The kids have to wait for now.'

'Then we'd best ride,' insisted Hawkins. 'The sooner we get there, the sooner I can make a try for the kids.'

Without another word they returned to their horses and set off towards the settlement, hoping they'd make it in time to do some good.

10

Gunter Lehringer stared in wide-eyed astonishment at the confused jumble of unshod pony tracks on the bank of the small stream that bordered his property. Despite the intense heat of the early morning, he suddenly felt a cold shiver run down his spine. A large band of Indians had crossed the stream and then turned north towards Medicine Bow. His keen eyes moved to the flies that were buzzing around a pile of soft horse dung on the other side of the narrow stream. The insects reaffirmed his belief that the sign was relatively fresh, probably no more than an hour or so old. There was no time to waste. The people at the settlement had to be warned.

Medicine Bow lay an hour's ride to the north, beyond a range of arid, rugged hills. The German knew the country like the back of his hand. The path he followed was steep and narrow with a broken, shaly surface with sheer drops on either side. Several times his mare almost lost her footing, but fortune smiled on him and he managed to keep control of the fretting animal. He was mighty relieved when they finally crested the hill and began the slightly easier descent to the valley floor below. At the bottom he paused briefly to check the lie of the land before kicking his mount into a desperate flat out gallop towards the settlement.

Sven Carlson was sweeping the wooden walkway in front of his store when he caught sight of a distant cloud of dust. He rested his arms on top of the broom handle and gazed towards the rapidly approaching rider. 'Someone's in a sure fired hurry to get here, by Jiminy,' he said aloud to no one in particular.

'What'd you say, Sven?' called Hank Masters, the settlement's blacksmith, from his forge directly across the dusty street.

'Rider coming in,' replied the jovial Swede, extending his right arm to point out the dust cloud. 'And he's riding like the Devil hisself is on his tail!' They stood their ground, waiting for the man to draw closer. 'That's ol' Lehringer!' exclaimed the Swede.

'Can't imagine what he wants here,' said Masters. Like everyone else in and around Medicine Bow, he had little time for the sheep farmer. Sheep rearers had never been popular in a territory where cattle was king. Back in '74 two Mexican immigrants who had brought their sheep with them across the border had been found hanging from the branch of a cottonwood tree just outside the settlement. The unsolved murders had turned Lehringer into even more of a lonely hermit. He only left the farm a few times a year, normally to buy essential supplies or to make arrangements for the sale of his spring lambs.

As the sheepman brought his lathered mount to a halt in front of the general store, Masters set aside his tools and stepped out into the street to see what all the fuss was about. 'This is an unexpected pleasure,' he sneered. 'To what do we owe this honour?'

Lehringer scowled at him. He knew he was unpopular, but he didn't care. 'You got plenty trouble coming,' he said, his eyes darting from one to the other.

'Vot do you mean?' enquired Carlson, with a worried frown.

'Vot I mean, Carlson, is that you folks are going to be visited by Apaches!'

Masters gave a deep, long belly laugh. 'Apaches!' he mocked. 'Lehringer, you been out in the sun too long, or maybe you been at the schnapps again.'

Lehringer shook his head. 'No, sir,' he insisted. 'I know vot I saw.'

'Joost vot did you see, Lehringer?' asked Carlson, stepping off the walkway to join him in the street.

'Yeah,' agreed Masters, 'what was it you saw, sheepman? A half-starved buck who'd skipped away from the reservation to hunt hisself a few rabbits?'

The farmer shook his head again. He sensed that they weren't going to listen to him. For a moment he contemplated turning his back on them, but he knew he had to tell them what he had seen. He sighed in frustration and tried again. 'Vot I saw vas the tracks of many unshod ponies on the banks of the stream close to my farm. They were heading this way.'

Carlson's demeanour instantly changed. 'Are you sure they were unshod ponies?'

The German nodded. 'I'm sure,' he insisted.

'Can't be,' argued Masters stubbornly, swatting irritably at a fly that was buzzing about his head. 'You probably seen the tracks of an army patrol.'

Genuine anger flared in the farmer's blue eyes as he glared at the blacksmith. 'I know the difference between army and Apache ponies,' he snapped.

'Go home and sleep it off, Lehringer,' sneered the blacksmith, tetchily. He had heard enough of the German's prevarications. 'You're either drunk or crazy, or both!'

The farmer ignored the jibe. He turned his back on the blacksmith and concentrated all his efforts on the big Swede. 'Vot about you, Carlson? Do you think I am seeing things?'

The storekeeper shook his head slowly from side to side. 'I don't know vot to think,' he admitted. 'But, by Jiminy, an Apache war party, it just don't seem likely, Lehringer.'

'You've said your piece,' interrupted the blacksmith. 'You've warned us. Now get out. We don't like havin' your kind around, stinks the place up worse than any Apache.'

'Stubborn fools,' said Lehringer, half under his breath. 'I should not have bothered.' Lehringer mounted his horse and brought her about. He looked back over his shoulder at Carlson and said, 'People may die here today.' With that he kicked his mare in the flanks and set off back to his farm. Although he felt both angry and frustrated his conscience was clear, for he had done his best to alert the stubborn inhabitants of Medicine Bow to the Apache menace. It was not his fault that they had chosen to ignore his warning.

Carlson stood silently in the middle of the street watching the farmer disappear into the distance. 'You don't think he could be right about an Apache war party?' he asked nervously.

'Not a cat in hell's chance,' replied Masters. 'Just forget about it.'

'Forget about what?' asked Frank Spencer, the manager of the stage and freight company office, as he joined them in the street.

The two men had been so engrossed in watching the German vanish into the hills that they had failed to hear him coming up behind them. They both turned to greet him with friendly smiles, though Spencer detected a momentary trace of anxiety in the Swede's face ahead of his grin. ' 'T'ain't nothin',' replied Masters casually.

'Sven?' pressed the stage-line manager, not at all certain that the blacksmith was levelling with him.

The storekeeper shrugged his massive shoulders. 'Lehringer just paid us a visit. He reckoned he'd seen sign of an Apache raiding party,' he advised.

'And I told him he was mistaken,' added the blacksmith.

Spencer instantly turned white as a ghost. 'What's up, Frank?' asked Carlson, somewhat alarmed by the look on his face.

'The stage,' replied the line manager.

'What about the friggin' stage?' enquired Masters irritably.

'It was due in last night,' he replied. 'And it still ain't showed up yet.'

'Stage is always late,' argued Masters. ' 'T'ain't nothin' to get het up about.'

'But it ain't ever this late!' stated Spencer, his eyes quickly darting from one to the other. 'I don't like the feel of this one little bit.'

'Quit worrying,' scolded the black-smith, shaking his head in exasperation. 'The stage'll be here soon enough. That damn Kraut's got you both spooked over nothin'.'

'Why would he lie?' asked Spencer, meeting the blacksmith's steely gaze. 'Did you ask yourself that? What would he have to gain? Go on tell me, what would he gain by it?'

'Frank makes a good point, by golly,' agreed Carlson. 'Vot would he gain?'

'Hell, I don't know,' replied Masters. 'Maybe he's just a lonely ol' man who wanted to make hisself look important.'

Spencer shook his head defiantly. 'That's plain horse-shit,' he said. 'And you know it.'

'The more I think on it, the more I reckon Lehringer must have really seen something the way he was acting up,' said Carlson.

'All reet, all reet,' screamed the blacksmith, throwing up this hands in mock surrender. 'Have it your own way.' He untied the strings on his black, leather apron, tore it testily from around his neck and strode off towards his shop. 'I'll go check it out. Maybe then ya'll be satisfied that there ain't no God-damned Apaches,' he yelled back at the top of his voice. A few minutes later he rode his dun around to the front and halted in front of the two men. 'This is a God-damned waste a time,' he said, spitting into the street. 'I'll be back in a couple of hours. If'n I find any Apaches, I'll bring you some hair to hang on your wall!' With that he turned the dun about and galloped off in the direction of the German's farm.

'Should we say anything to the others?' asked Carlson, as he watched his friend disappear into a gathering cloud of dust.

Spencer nodded. 'Yeah,' he replied. 'I'm a mite concerned about scarin' folks without just cause, but I don't like the smell of this. Let's get everyone into the church. It'll be the best place to make a stand if'n we are attacked.'

11

With unfamiliar smells and sounds from within the house registering deep in his subconscious mind, Chato finally began the slow ascent out of his fever-induced sleep. When he first opened his eyes and tried to raise his head, he felt so weak that he immediately slumped back down on to the soft, damp cot. Where was he? What had happened to him? Everything about his surroundings was strange and frightening. Then, as he lay gazing upwards, he suddenly realized why. His eyes were looking at the shingled roof of a white-eye's house. It was then that he heard a female voice speak softly to him in the language of the Mexicans. 'Don't be afraid,' said the voice. 'No one here will hurt you.'

Chato slowly turned his head towards the strange-sounding voice. He recoiled in fear when he caught sight of the smiling face of a white woman. As she moved slowly across the room towards him he tried to withdraw into the wall at his back.

'Are you hungry?' she enquired calmly. He shook his head slowly. Fear and suspicion glowed in his dark eyes. 'A doctor fixed your wound,' she advised. His hand instinctively went to his injured shoulder. He gave a slight grimace but otherwise successfully managed to mask his pain. 'Please eat some broth,' she said. 'It will help you regain your strength.' When he gave a curt, nervous nod she made her way to the stove. Lucy moved swiftly to her mama's side and then clung tightly on to her skirt tail as she strolled across the room to feed her wary patient.

'Who are you?' he croaked weakly, still not convinced about her good intentions.

Carefully choosing the right words, in her somewhat rusty Spanish, she answered his question and then offered him the bowl.

He took it awkwardly from her with his left hand. Ignoring the proffered spoon, he put it to his lips and took a dubious sip. Satisfied that it wasn't poisoned, he took another swallow of the hot broth, grimacing against a sudden sharp stab of pain in his injured shoulder.

'He ain't got no manners, Mama,' said little Lucy indignantly, peering around Nancy's hips. 'He slurps his food like a hog!'

'He hasn't got any manners,' corrected her mama good-naturedly. 'But it's rude to criticize him,' she added. 'For he's hurt and scared.'

'What's he scared of, Mama?'

'Us, Lucy, us!'

'What are you saying?' asked Chato with a scowl, setting the empty bowl in his lap.

'My daughter was asking why you are scared of us,' she replied.

'Chato is afraid of no one!' he

exclaimed. 'Least of all a white woman and her child.'

Nancy grinned. 'I'm glad to hear it,' she chuckled. With that she turned her back on the youngster and swept away with Lucy in tow to take care of the morning chores.

Around mid-morning, Tod Gates decided he was sorely in need of a cup of coffee. He put aside the rake he had been using to clean out the soiled hay from the stalls inside the barn, ran a sleeve across his warm, moist brow and strode to the door calling out to Johnny that he'd be right back. The blistering heat and sweltering humidity in the open were almost overpowering. He paused in front of the house to dip his head into the water trough. When he came upright again he shook his head from side to side and then ran his fingers through his thick, matted hair. It was then that his keen eyes noticed the rising cloud of dust a mile or so off to the west. 'Johnny!' he yelled, at the top of his voice.

'Yeah, Pa?' called the youngster, moving to the open doorway of the barn.

'Get in the house, boy,' instructed his pa.

'But I ain't finished my chores yet.'

'Don't argue, boy. Just do as I say and be quick about it.'

Johnny shrugged his shoulders, rested his rake up against the wall of the barn and walked over to join his pa by the trough. 'What's up, Pa?' he asked with a frown.

'Probably nothin',' replied his pa, resting a hand on the boy's shoulder. 'But 'til we knows for sure just who's come a' callin' we'll keep a watch from behind our walls.' With that he led his son inside the house. 'Close the shutters at the back,' he ordered Johnny, as he barred the front door behind him.

'What is it, Tod?' asked Nancy from the kitchen table, where she was mixing dough.

'We got visitors,' he replied pulling

the shutters closed across the front windows. It was then that he noticed the boy sitting up in the cot on the far side of the room. 'I see he's awake,' he said. 'Guess we'll have to watch our backs as well as our fronts!' He checked that both his rifle and handgun were fully loaded and then moved swiftly to the spyhole he had bored through the stout wooden door at the front of the house. 'Quit your cookin', Nancy,' he ordered calmly, 'and pick up the Henry. Johnny, keep watch at the back.'

A moment later they heard the drumming of hoofbeats. 'Apaches,' muttered Tod Gates. His heart started to race as he took in the dark-skinned warriors who had reined in a hundred yards from the front of the house. He counted nineteen. They sat motionless astride their lathered ponies, staring silently at the house, wearing their traditional clothing of coloured headbands, breech clouts and knee-length animal hide boots. The bright streaks of red, yellow and black war paint that adorned their faces gave them a surreal and menacing appearance. 'Johnny,' he called sharply, 'anything movin' out back?'

'No, Pa,' replied the boy, putting his eye to the loophole in the wall.

'Can we stand them off?' asked Nancy, moving to her husband's side with the Henry rifle clasped tightly in her trembling hands.

'I ain't rightly sure,' he said quietly. 'But if'n they get inside the house, you know what to do.' She nodded.

Nancy was halfway to her defensive position on the other side of the door when a noise like the Devil's choir filled the air. Shrieking and whooping at the tops of their voices the Apaches surged forward *en masse*. They circled the house firing rifles and arrows from beneath their ponies' necks. Dozens of bullets whined and pinged as they bounced harmlessly off the outer walls. Two of the windows shattered under the gunfire, but the inner wooden

116

shutters protected the occupants of the house from flying glass.

Gates and his family returned fire but found it impossible to hit any of the swiftly moving raiders through the dust churned up by their whirling mounts. A cacophony of exploding gunfire, thundering hooves and spine-tingling warcries filled the air. The noise both inside and outside the house was deafening. Inside the hot, stuffy room the desperate defenders began to cough and splutter in response to smoke and the smell of sulphur from their barking guns as they maintained a murderous fire to keep the Apaches at bay.

Two raiders broke away from the main band and rode behind the barn. They quickly dismounted out of sight of the house and set fire to the rear wall. The dry wood instantly caught alight. In a matter of minutes the crackling, spitting flames had spread to the hayloft. Acrid black smoke billowed skywards.

An angry Tod Gates cursed aloud and then took careful aim at a palomino pony as it came into sight from behind the blazing barn. He squeezed the trigger slowly and absorbed the heavy recoil of the rifle in his powerful shoulder. The horse gave a loud whinny and collapsed to the ground, spilling its rider into the dirt thirty feet from the house. Before the rancher could get off another shot, the Apache sprang to his feet and gratefully grabbed the outstretched hand of another warrior as he galloped past. He was lifted up behind the rider in one graceful, effortless movement and whisked away to safety. The rancher swore again as he swung his heavy rifle to fire at another of the other raiders. His hurried shot went high and wide.

Having tested their enemies' fire, the raiders broke off their assault and withdrew to rest their panting mounts and reassess the situation. The only casualty they had suffered was one dead pony. In return they had forced the defenders to waste a good deal of their precious ammunition. They also knew exactly how many guns they were up against. Their leader, a dumpy, squat figure with hawk-like features and cruel, black eyes sat astride his black and white pony studying the ranch house. After a few minutes of silent contemplation he issued a series of short rapid commands, which he illustrated with animated hand gestures. The warriors immediately wheeled their mounts about and formed up to resume the attack.

Tod Gates gave a loud, raspy cough. He waved his hand in front of his face to disperse some of the lingering smoke from his hot rifle and then gazed out of his loophole. His heart was beating rapidly and he was sweating profusely. Every window in the house was broken and both the front and back doors were studded with arrows and war lances. But the damage was purely superficial. The house remained solid and defiant. But with more than half their ammunition expended and no enemy losses to speak of the question that burned in the rancher's mind was how much longer could they hold out?

It was then that a young voice spoke out boldly in Spanish from the far side of the room. 'They will set fire to the roof,' said Chato, his face showing no trace of emotion.

'What'd he say?' asked Gates, turning to face his wife.

'I must go to them,' said Chato.

'You will stop them?' asked Nancy, turning to face the boy.

'Yes,' he replied, fighting back his pain and discomfort.

Nancy turned to face her frustrated husband. 'He says he will help us,' she said.

'And you believe him?'

'Yes,' she replied firmly. 'I think I do.'

'Well I sure as hell don't!'

'Tod,' she insisted, 'you know they'll burn us out. For God's sake, think about the kids. I'll try anything to save them right now.' She stared at him appealingly. 'Please, Tod!'

He let out a sigh. 'Have it your own way,' he said. 'But I still say it's a big mistake.'

She hurried across the room to help Chato out of bed. Tod Gates shook his head, leaned his rifle against the wall and then slid the heavy wooden plank away from the slats that held it in place across the door.

'You ain't goin' out there with him,' he insisted, blocking her path. 'He'll have to make it on his own.'

'He can't,' she replied, pausing just short of the door. 'He can hardly stand.'

'This is pure foolishness,' he snapped, unable to contain his anger. He took the boy from his wife with a scowl. 'Johnny,' he called, over his shoulder.

'Yeah, Pa?'

'Get over here and open the door. Then help your ma to keep watch at the front.'

The Apaches were about to resume

the attack when they became aware of people moving about on the porch at the front of the house. They could clearly recognize the boy as one of their own. This unexpected development aroused their curiosity. The leader of the raiding party raised a hand to silence the warriors. 'They wish to talk.' he said. 'Kayitah, Alchise, you will ride down with me to speak to the whites.'

'It might be a trick, Victorio,' observed Alchise.

'At the first sign of treachery we will open fire.'

They cantered up to the house and reined in a few feet away. Their eyes quickly swept the area for any sign of danger. 'We could kill them all now with ease,' whispered Kayitah, as he locked eyes with the rancher on the porch.

'No,' insisted Victorio. 'Alchise, you speak the white-man's tongue, ask him why he holds the boy prisoner?' The warrior immediately did as he was told.

Tod Gates had never felt so scared in his entire life, but he managed to mask his fear as he gazed into the black, hate-filled eyes of the savage who addressed him. But before he could offer a reply, the young boy he supported spoke up in the language of his own people. 'These whites helped me when I was hurt,' he said.

'Since when has a white been a friend to the Apache?' growled Victorio.

'They could have let me die,' insisted the boy.

Gates, who had no idea what was being said, looked nervously at each of the Apaches in turn and prayed that he could get to the pistol on his hip if trouble flared.

'How are you called?' asked Victorio, sternly. 'And how did you come to be here?'

Chato told him everything he needed to know.

Victorio gave a curt nod and then paused for a moment to take it all in. He then turned to Alchise and said,

'Tell the white man my name and then translate my words.'

Alchise nodded and turned to face the rancher. 'The mighty Victorio will speak with you through me.'

'Victorio!' Gates exclaimed. The mere mention of the war chief's name made the hairs on the back of his neck stand on end. He stared hard at the middleaged warrior in front of him and shook his head in disbelief.

'You know of me?' asked the chief. Gates nodded. It brought a smile to the chief's face. 'Tell him I hold his life in the palm of my hand, like a grain of sand,' instructed Victorio, opening his right hand to the sky.

'I ain't afeard,' replied Gates, his face expressionless. 'You may kill me, but many Apache will die too before you claim my scalp.' Alchise promptly translated his defiant words.

Victorio grinned. 'It is good you are not afraid to die,' he said, pausing for Alchise to do his work. 'The Apache respects a brave enemy. But today we will not kill.' He looked deep into the rancher's soul before continuing his speech. 'You spared the life of an Apache boy, you are healing him, for this I give you back your life. No Apache will harm you or your family while the boy remains here. But when he is well he must return to his people. When he goes, you will leave also, for this is Apache land! We want no whites here.'

When Alchise had finished translating, Victorio gave a loud whoop, wheeled his mount about and galloped back towards the warriors who were waiting on the far side of the burning barn. Kayitah went with him, but Alchise remained behind. 'Listen well, white eyes,' he snarled. 'Today you have much luck. I would have killed you now. But we will be back, and next time my knife will take your life, one piece at a time.'

'I'll be ready, boy,' sneered Gates, as the Apache rode off to join his companions. He let out a sigh of relief, turned on his heels and helped Chato back into the house. Although he held no love for the boy, he was truly grateful for his intervention. Chato's words had bought safety for the Gates family, at least for the time being.

12

It took a lot of persuasion to cajole the inhabitants of Medicine Bow into swapping their daily chores for a spell in the church. The majority of the menfolk were highly sceptical about the warning and argued long and hard with Carlson and Spencer. A number of voices were raised in anger and on one occasion violence briefly threatened. However, common sense eventually prevailed and within the hour every man, woman, child and horse had crossed the river to take up sanctuary in the church. They took with them plenty of guns, ammunition and food to see them through any protracted siege.

The women and children immediately took up residence within the cool walls of the imposing building. Father Thomas O'Farrell, the local padre, encouraged them to pray for their salvation. While he spoke, Frank Spencer climbed the narrow, winding steps to stand guard in the square-shaped bell tower, cradling a Winchester in his hands. The rest of the men remained outside the church: some smoking, a few idly talking, but a good many moaning about the stupidity of wasting the best part of the day when they had work to do.

Carlson ignored the barbed comments uttered by his cantankerous neighbours as he stood defiantly by the double-fronted, solid oak doors of the church, keeping a watchful eye on the shimmering horizon. He shook his head in amazement at how unconcerned most of them seemed to be about the potential danger. There was time when the word 'Apache' would have started a genuine panic. Now the idea of a raid brought only laughter and derision.

From his vantage point forty feet above the ground, Frank Spencer put a hand to his forehead and squinted through the fierce glare of the sun at the unchanging land. Nothing moved for as far as the eye could see. His check cotton shirt was soaked through with perspiration, making him feel most uncomfortable. Having dabbed at his sweaty brow with a handkerchief, he removed his hat and used it as fan. He felt badly in need of a cool drink, but before descending to ground level to quench his thirst, he paused by the parapet to take one last sweep of the land. When his eyes came to rest on a long, grassy embankment half a mile beyond the stream his heart skipped a beat. Menacingly silhouetted against the blue skyline were more than twenty dusky, mounted figures. 'Apaches!' he exclaimed in a croaky voice.

'Vot did you say, Frank?' queried Carlson, lifting his head towards the tower.

Spencer swallowed hard to clear his throat. 'Apaches!' he yelled. This time everyone heard him. Anxious faces turned towards the river just as ghastly, blood-curdling war whoops echoed across the land. The Apaches were already charging down the slope towards them.

'Oh, God!' said Hal Lines, one of the local ranchers. 'We're dead!'

'Everyone inside the church,' ordered Carlson, galvanizing everyone into action. 'Quickly, quickly. Horses too.' They slammed the heavy doors shut behind them, plunging the building into semi-darkness. The only natural light came from the five open windows cut out of the stonework along the east and west walls of the church, eight feet above ground level.

Counting the padre, there were eight men present. There were also six women and eleven children: eight girls and three boys, ranging in age from six months to fourteen years.

Carlson immediately took charge. He put the padre in charge of the women and children, who were all huddled up close together by the north wall. Two men were despatched to the bell tower to help Spencer. The store-keeper and the others then quickly set about stacking the heavy wooden pews up against the east and west walls in order to form three platforms from which to fire down from the high windows.

By the time the men clambered awkwardly into position to return fire, the Apaches were already circling the church at a distance of twenty yards. One bold, half-naked savage whose animated face was daubed with black streaks of war paint suddenly kicked his pony towards the doors at the front of the church. When he was ten feet from the building he reined in, forcing his mount up on to its hind legs, and hurled a feathered lance at the door. It slammed into the woodwork with a loud, quivering thump. The snarling Apache then swung his pony about and galloped away out of range of the defenders' guns.

The encircling warriors concentrated their efforts on the doors at the front of the church. A number of flaming arrows were sent thudding into their target as the bucks tore on past. The guns in the tower kept up a withering fire which helped to keep the determined Apaches at bay. But the defenders were businessmen, craftsmen and ranchers, not skilled gunmen. For all their combined efforts they only managed to bring down two Apache ponies. On both occasions the downed Indians were swiftly picked up uninjured and carried off to safety.

Inside the church the deafening noise and acrid smell from the guns caused a few of the younger children to start crying. Equally terrified mothers put on brave faces and tried to reassure their offspring that everything would be all right. When the battle was at its fiercest, the two boys who carried guns exchanged nervous glances. Although they didn't say a word, the same thought occupied both their troubled minds: would they be able to carry out Carlson's orders if the Apaches gained entry to the building? The worried Swede had taken them aside just prior to climbing up to his defensive position atop the pews. He had warned them what would happen to the women and children if they were taken alive. Keeping his voice low, he had instructed the shocked boys to kill them all should the need arise. 'It will be a terribly hard thing for you to do,' he had said, 'but it will be a blessed kindness.' They had merely nodded and returned to their posts, hoping their resolve would never be put to the test. Now, as the Apaches tightened the noose, they began to wonder if they might have to face up to the daunting prospect sooner rather than later.

Mary Spencer, the wife of the stage-line manager, cradled her six-month-old baby in her trembling arms and tried to hush his crying. She and her husband had only just moved out West. When he got the job with the stage-line and told her they were leaving Missouri she had been a little anxious about living amongst the Indians. But once friends and relations had assured her that Apache raids were a thing of the past she began to share his dream of a new life in the Arizona territory, far from their run-down farm. Until the moment she had heard those awful shrieking warriors galloping towards the church she had never had cause to regret their move. Now the frail-looking, brown-haired, somewhat pretty girl wished she had never heard of Arizona.

The frenzied attack lasted only a few minutes, but to the people holed up inside the hot, stinking church it seemed like an eternity. When the Apaches broke off the engagement and withdrew across the stream the defenders in the tower wasted a good deal of valuable ammunition in trying to hit the retreating riders. Only when Carlson screamed at them from the foot of the steps did they cease firing. 'Keep a look-out,' he instructed, as an eerie silence finally descended on the world beyond their walls, 'we are going to open the doors and put out the fire.'

While his companions lifted the beam from its bracket, Carlson quickly pulled the double-doors open to inspect the damage. The dry wood was scorched from the effects of the flaming arrows that were embedded in the doors. He accepted a bucket of water from the concerned looking padre and doused the small flames. Jed Gessner, the local carpenter, stepped forward to remove the feathered war lance that was stuck fast in the left-hand door. He discarded it with an air of disgust. 'If'n that's the best they can manage I reckon we'll stand them off,' he growled, pulling the doors closed behind him.

'We ain't seen nothing yet, by golly,' Carlson told his companions. 'Those Apaches are just testing us out, seeing how many guns we have and where our weaknesses are.'

'We made it purty hot for 'em,' insisted Gessner, removing his thick spectacles to wipe a bead of perspiration from his brow. 'Maybe they won't come back.'

'They will be back,' stated Carlson firmly. 'Apaches don't give up so easy. They'll keep probing and trying to wear us down.'

'Let 'em come,' snapped Gessner's twenty-year-old son, Tom. 'They ain't likely to get through these walls in a hurry.'

'Somit's happening across the stream,' yelled Spencer from the tower, his words echoing eerily off the stone walls. 'You wanna come on up and take a looksee, Sven?'

'I'm on the way,' answered Carlson, turning away from his companions by the door.

By the time he reached the top of the tower he was breathing hard. He paused for a moment to catch his breath and then ducked his head into the gap between the sloping, tiled roof and the parapet to look at the activity beyond the stream. 'What're them red devils up to now?' asked

Spencer, moving to his friend's side.

'Oh, dear God! No, no,' cried Carlson, as his eyes fell on the ragged, bloody figure of Hank Masters mounted on a black horse between two stone-faced Apaches. The blacksmith's hands were bound behind him, his shirt was ripped and he had wounds to both his upper body and forehead. His captors reined in just out of rifle range on the far bank of the stream. Having quickly dismounted, they hauled their semi-conscious prisoner out of the saddle and dumped him unceremoniously on the ground at their feet.

'It's Hank,' said Spencer. 'The bastards have got Hank! We gotta do somit!'

'There's nothing we can do,' replied Carlson, as a wagon suddenly rattled into view. Just for a second he thought some unexpected help from one of the local ranches might have arrived, but the sight of the Apache driver and escort instantly dashed his hopes.

The wagon pulled to a halt right

behind the crumpled figure of Hank Masters. The Apaches immediately lifted him bodily to his feet and dragged him backwards to the front wheel of the wagon. Swiftly they bound his feet together and then strapped his arms to the wheel. The other Apaches who had ridden escort from the settlement went into the back of the wagon and brought out armfuls of wood and sagebrush which they placed at the blacksmith's feet and all around the front wheel. 'They're gonna burn him alive!' yelled Spencer, hardly able to believe what was happening. 'We can't just stand here and watch!'

Carlson grabbed hold of him by the arm as he made to leave. 'There's nothing we can do for him,' he said sadly. 'They are out of range of our guns.'

'I'm going out to help him,' insisted Spencer, pulling himself free.

'That's just what the Apaches are hoping you will do,' said Carlson. 'The minute you're outside they will cut you down and rush the door. They will get us all.'

'But he's my friend,' pleaded Spencer, desperately. 'I can't just let him die.'

'You're not going,' snapped Carlson, stepping towards him. Spencer instantly brought up his Winchester and levelled it at the store-keeper's midriff.

'Keep back, Sven,' he screeched. 'I don't want to hurt you, but if'n you try to stop me I swear I'll put a bullet in you.'

'For heaven's sake, Frank, please think about what you're doing,' pleaded Carlson. 'You'll only get yourself killed and endanger the rest of us into the bargain.'

'Bar the door behind me,' he said. 'Then y'all be safe.'

'You'll have to shoot me, Frank,' said the Swede, pressing his big belly up against the muzzle of the rifle. 'I'm not going to let you go out there.' The other two men in the tower began to edge slowly towards Spencer in the hope of getting around behind him unnoticed. But he caught sight of them out of the corner of his eye.

'Stay where you are!' he yelled, with a maniacal look in his eyes. Instantly they obeyed, fearing that their crazed companion would do something stupid. Spencer locked eyes with Carlson and rammed the barrel of his Winchester savagely into his friend's stomach. 'Back up, Sven,' he urged. 'Don't make me shoot you.'

'I'm not letting you go,' insisted Carlson defiantly.

Without warning, Spencer swung the barrel of his gun like a club into the side of the Swede's head. Carlson staggered back a pace and then collapsed to the stone floor, an angry purple graze forming on his temple.

'Don't move,' ordered Spencer, bringing his rifle to bear on the other two men.

'You're crazy,' said Ben Potts. 'You'll end up getting us all killed.'

'I ain't gonna argue the point no

more,' growled Spencer. 'Now, do as I tell you.'

'Let him go, Ben,' said Luke Tatchpole, the fourth man in the tower. 'It's his funeral. If he wants to get hisself killed, then let him go right ahead.'

Potts let out a long, defeated sigh. 'All reet, Spencer,' he agreed, 'have it your own way. We'll try and cover you from up here.'

Spencer kept his gun on them as he moved towards the steps. Within seconds he was lifting the cross-beam from the double doors at the front of the church. Ignoring the questions and protests of the frightened men and women all about him, he pulled the doors open and said, 'Bar the doors behind me, but be ready to open up when you hear me holler.'

'For God's sake, Frank,' implored Mary, crossing the floor towards him carrying their infant son in her arms, 'what are you trying to do?'

He turned his head towards his

terrified wife and said, 'I ain't got time to argue, Mary. This is just something I have to do.' Without another word he disappeared outside.

Before he had covered half a dozen steps the air was filled with the most awful, pain-racked screams he had ever heard. He halted not thirty feet from the church and gazed at the burning wagon on the other side of the stream. Bright yellow and red flames were shooting up all around his helpless, struggling friend. Masters' clothing was already alight. Spencer roared his anger at the sky and set off at a dead run towards the wagon. Before he got halfway, a dozen whooping Apaches charged the church, cutting off his line of retreat. A rapid burst of answering gunfire came from the tower, but the savages maintained their attack.

The Apaches standing guard, ran to their ponies and prepared to meet the advance of the crazed white man. When he saw them riding towards him, Spencer knew what he had to do. He went down on one knee, raised his rifle to his shoulder and sighted along the barrel at his helpless friend. His hands were shaking as his finger tightened around the trigger. Sweat trickled down from his forehead to sting his eyes. He swallowed hard, said a silent prayer for his tormented friend and then absorbed the recoil as the rifle bucked in his hands. Fortunately, his aim was true and Masters' suffering was brought to a merciful end.

The infuriated Apaches waded the stream and made a beeline for Spencer. Their bullets sent puffs of dust spiralling up into the air all around him as he stood up to meet their advance. He shouldered his rifle once more and returned fire. One of his hurried shots caught the leading Apache in the chest. He toppled backwards off his horse to lie still in the grass. The second buck howled his rage and let loose an arrow on the gallop. It produced a curious whistling sound as it flew through the air to bury itself deep in Spencer's right shoulder. The force of the blow caused him to drop his rifle and fall to his knees.

Frank Spencer knew he was about to die. Pain clouded his eyes as he grasped hold of the feathered shaft. As the realization sank in he was surprised to find that he didn't really fear death. His only regret was that he would never see his wife and baby son again. It was only then that he began to appreciate how selfish he had been. He had rashly thrown away his life and in so doing had deprived his loved ones of a husband and father. But it was too late, far too late for self-recrimination or pity. But there was time for one last act of defiance as the gleeful Apache closed in for the kill. He reached down for the pistol on his hip, pulled it clear of its leather holster, fanned back the hammer, put the muzzle to his temple and pulled the trigger.

'God damn,' sighed Luke Tatchpole from his vantage point in the tower.

'Dumb bastard never stood a chance,'

remarked Potts, with a sad shake of his head. He looked down at Carlson, who was sitting up with his back up against the outer wall of the tower, his eyes firmly closed and his head in his hands, and said, 'How you doin', Sven?'

The Swede was feeling very much the worse for wear. In his woozy, concussed state he had no idea of what was going on around him. 'Vot?' he asked, dimly.

'You gonna be OK big fella?' asked Tatchpole, laying a friendly hand on his shoulder.

Carlson groaned as he forced his eyes open. He looked up vacantly at his two companions and said, 'Vot happened to me?' Tatchpole immediately told him.

'You don't look so good, Sven,' observed Potts. 'Maybe you should go lie down for a spell and get your strength back while you can?'

Carlson peered up at the two men through glazed eyes and said, 'Help me up.' They took hold of him under the armpits, lifted him gently back to his feet and led him downstairs.

In the far corner of the church Mary Spencer sat cradling her baby, weeping quietly, her head resting against the comforting shoulder of Annabel Lines. The rancher's wife had known more than her own share of grief down the years. She stroked the young widow's hair gently and softly tried to reassure her that she was amongst friends who would help her through her ordeal. But Mary Spencer never heard a single word she said. Shock had taken her into a private world, far away, where no one could reach her. She was still sheltering there, oblivious to everything going on around her, when the cry went up that the Apaches were renewing their attack.

13

Sam Hawkins raised no objection when Wheeler decided to travel to Medicine Bow via the Gates's ranch. They were less than a mile from his brother-in-law's spread when Wheeler caught the faint trace of wood-smoke in the still air. His hand fell to the Winchester poking out of the saddleboot by his right knee. Pulling it free, he levered a round into the chamber and set off at a canter towards the ranch, hoping that he wasn't too late to help his kinfolk.

The sound of their approach brought Johnny to the porch. 'We had some visitors while you was gone,' announced the youngster excitedly.

'How'd y'all manage to drive 'em off?' asked Wheeler, as he dismounted.

'We didn't,' advised Tod Gates, as he emerged from the house. 'If'n it hadn't been for the Apache boy our scalps would probably be dangling from a war lance right now.'

'What happened?' pressed Wheeler. The rancher quickly told him the whole story.

'And where's that stinkin' Apache now?' growled Hawkins.

'Inside,' replied Gates, with a frown.

'His people murdered my kin,' snapped the vet. 'Now I reckon to even the score.'

'Hold up, Hawkins,' growled Wheeler, grabbing hold of the man by the arm as he tried to push past him. 'He ain't done you no harm; there ain't no call to take your hate out on him.'

'Stay away from me,' barked Hawkins, pulling free of the scout's grip. Before Wheeler could react, Hawkins pulled his gun and pistol-whipped him across the temple. As Wheeler collapsed with a loud groan, Gates instinctively threw himself on to the vet's back, pinning his arms to his side. His forward momentum caused them to trip over the prostrate scout. They ended up in a tangled heap beyond the porch, wrestling for possession of the Navy Colt, while Johnny stood transfixed in the open doorway, too frightened to move. Although the rancher had a considerable weight advantage, his opponent fought like a wildcat. Suddenly, in the middle of the desperate struggle, the gun went off. Gates cried out in pain and keeled over on to his side.

'Nooo . . . ' cried Johnny. He dashed from the doorway to kneel beside his stricken pa.

Hawkins climbed awkwardly to his feet and stared down at the crumpled figure on the ground. 'I warned you, Tod!' he screamed. 'I warned you, but you wouldn't listen.'

He thumbed back the hammer on the Colt and, turning his back on the rancher, strode purposefully towards the house. An enraged, tearful Johnny sprang to his feet with all the speed and grace of a young puma. Without a thought for his own safety, he threw himself at Hawkins, locking the crook of his left arm around his neck and holding on for dear life. Hawkins twisted one way and then the other in his frantic attempts to shake him off. Finally, he got a firm grip on the youngster's head, forcing him to let go of his neck. Hawkins dumped the spunky kid on his butt in the dirt and then spun around to grab hold of him again by the hair, dragging him back to his feet. Johnny squealed in pain and anger as Hawkins slapped him brutally across the face. The youngster fell sobbing to his knees, his hands covering his stinging face.

'You shot my pa,' he cried, as Hawkins picked up his gun. 'You're a murderer!'

'You shouldn't have done that, Sam,' advised Nancy from the open doorway, as she stepped around her woozy brother. The Henry rifle she carried caused him to freeze on the spot.

'Put the gun down,' he hissed,

keeping a wary eye on Johnny as he came to his feet.

'I won't let you kill the Apache boy,' she stated, firmly. 'Now drop your pistol or I swear I'll shoot.'

'You ain't got the nerve,' he said, taking a step towards her. He managed one step before the slug hit him. The sudden burning sensation in his chest halted him in his tracks. He dropped his pistol and stared in disbelief at the red stain that was spreading across his shirt.

'You should have listened to me,' said Nancy, shaking her head. 'As God's my witness, I told you I'd do it.' His knees gave way and he toppled on to his face in the dirt.

A frightened looking Chato appeared in the doorway behind Nancy. He had heard the commotion from his sickbed and had sensed that it meant trouble for him. Almost immediately he was joined by a tearful Lucy.

'It's all over,' stated Nancy calmly, in Spanish. 'He can't hurt you now.'

151

She rested the rifle against the wall of the house and went to help her husband. As she did so, her brother climbed rather unsteadily to his feet. 'Go get me a bowl of water and some clean rags,' she said to Johnny.

Tod Gates opened his eyes and grinned at his wife. 'Did you get him, gal?'

'Yeah,' she replied, returning his smile. 'I got him.'

'Is Johnny OK?' She nodded. 'What about the Apache kid?' She nodded again. 'Help me into the house,' he said, encouraging his wife to give him a hand up. They made it to the porch just as Johnny reappeared carrying a bowl of water and some clean rag. Wheeler came forward to meet them. 'Are you hurt bad?' he enquired, rubbing his own throbbing head.

'Could be worse,' replied Gates. 'Let's get inside and talk.'

After cleaning and dressing her husband's wound, Nancy turned her attention to her brother. The fracas had left him with a pounding headache and had also reopened the hole in his side. Nancy carefully unwrapped the bandage and examined the weeping wound. 'Ouch!' he exclaimed, trying to pull away.

'Quit squawking,' she said with a broad grin. 'Let me do my work.'

When she had finished, she wrapped a fresh bandage tightly around his midriff. 'You all done now?' he asked with a hint of sarcasm.

She just grinned. 'You'll do,' she said, standing up and moving away from the table with a swish of her blue gingham dress.

'What d'you figure on doin' now?' asked Tod Gates, wincing with pain as he crossed the room awkwardly to sit down opposite his brother-in-law.

They spent several minutes discussing their various options. The one thing they agreed on was the need to help the people at the settlement. Wheeler was caught between riding for aid or going on to the township to help organize their defences. He knew that his experience in fighting the Apaches could make a crucial difference to the settlers' chances of survival. That was why he eventually proposed that it should be left to young Johnny to seek help.

'Come on, Ty, you can't be serious?' replied a bemused Gates. 'You wanna send a kid to do a man's job?'

'We don't have a choice,' said Wheeler, 'You ain't up to the ride and Nancy needs to stay put and look after y'all. That only leaves Johnny.'

'I can do it,' said Johnny enthusiastically. 'I can, Pa, I ain't scared.'

'No,' insisted the rancher firmly. 'I won't hear of it, it's too dangerous.'

'It ain't a thing I suggest lightly,' said Wheeler. 'But he only needs to go as far as Joe Brady's spread on the Gila. Ole Joe'll send one of his buckaroos on to the fort and Johnny can hole up at his place until I come for him.'

Gates rose slowly and stiffly from his chair, put a hand on his throbbing side and made his way across the room to gaze absentmindedly out of the window at the scorched grassland and the distant craggy hills. 'All reet,' he agreed reluctantly, with a resigned sigh, turning back to face his brother-in-law. 'Johnny, you'll take my sorrel. Go saddle up. Your ma'll pack you some grub for the ride.' The excited youngster hurtled out of the door before his pa could change his mind.

Johnny reappeared in the house just as his uncle finished writing a note to Brady. Wheeler called him over and stuffed the letter into his shirt pocket. 'Give that to Joe Brady,' he said. 'And then stay put until I come for you.'

'But I wanna come on home,' argued the boy, with a pained expression.

'You'll do as you're told, boy,' instructed his pa from across the room. 'Now collect your grub, kiss your ma goodbye and get a'goin', pronto.'

Wheeler rose from his seat and strolled across the room to speak to Chato, who had maintained a stoic silence throughout the lengthy discussions. His eyes came alert as the scout halted a foot from the bed. 'I have to go away again for a while,' he said. 'You'll be safe here until I return.'

'You go to fight Victorio?' asked Chato, locking eyes with the scout. Wheeler gave him a rueful smile and shrugged his shoulders. 'He will kill you.'

Wheeler turned his back on the boy and strode off towards the door, collecting his rifle on the way. Once outside he moved to Johnny's side and gave him a leg up on to the sorrel. 'You got nothin' to worry about, kid,' he advised with a reassuring smile. 'There ain't nothin' out there but grass.'

'I ain't afeard,' replied the youngster.

'I know you ain't,' grinned Wheeler, patting the boy lightly on the leg. 'Just head due east 'til you hit the hills and then turn north. It'll take you about five to six hours. Keep your wits about you and remember everything you've been taught.'

The youngster smiled down at his anxious parents and little sister and then wheeled his mount about. With a carefree wave, he set off across the grassy plain towards the distant, shimmering hills. Wheeler moved swiftly away to his own horse. He gave a half-suppressed grunt of pain as he clambered awkwardly into the saddle. 'Stay close, Tod. Don't take any chances,' he said, as he set off towards the settlement, hoping he would be in time to help them.

14

From his position in the bell tower, Ben Potts shielded his eyes from the glare of the sun and peered at the gathering dust cloud far to the north of the river. A tingle of excitement ran down his spine. The swirling dust could only mean one thing: help was at hand. He yelled at the top of his lungs for Carlson to come up and join him.

'Vot is it? Vot's all the excitement?' queried the store-keeper, fighting to catch his breath, as he reached the top step of the tower. When Potts pointed towards the river, he squinted through the glare and said, 'A lot of riders, by golly.'

'Yeah,' said Luke Tatchpole, as he sauntered over to join them, 'but them Apach' don't look too concerned to me.'

'God damn!' exclaimed Carlson,

swinging back to face the approaching riders. 'No wonder they ain't worried.' Instead of the anticipated cavalry patrol they found themselves staring at another band of mounted Apaches.

'What the hell do we do now?' groaned Potts. 'There must be forty or more, all told.'

'Nothin's changed,' insisted Carlson defiantly. 'We will just hold our ground and wait until help comes.'

'And what if it don't come?'

Before his companion could frame an answer, the chilling sound of shrill warcries filled the air. Fifty yards from the church, the Apaches fanned out to attack on all sides. Within a matter of seconds they had tightened their circle, drawing ever closer to the walls of the old church.

The defenders manning the open windows returned fire, desperately trying to pick their targets amongst the swirling cloud of dust that rapidly enveloped the precincts of the church.

'Don't let 'em git to the doors!'

yelled Tatchpole, raising his head to draw a bead on a daring half-naked warrior who was making a beeline for the front of the church. But before he could pull the trigger a bullet hit him right between the eyes. His two companions were sprayed with bright crimson blood as he fell backwards to land in a crumpled heap.

Carlson wiped the blood from his face and, taking great care to expose as little of himself as possible, began to return fire. Potts coughed and spluttered loudly, took a deep breath, shook his head violently from side to side, gave an angry roar and followed Carlson's example.

The battle raged on unabated for what seemed like an eternity. When the doors at the front of the building caught fire, they were forced to act. Hal Lines grabbed a bucket of water and screamed at two of his fellow defenders to open the doors and provide him with cover. Carlson and Potts were well aware of what was happening down below. They concentrated their fire on the Apaches at the front of the building. Together with the two men flanking Lines they managed to keep the raiders at bay while he quickly doused the flames.

A mile or so to the north, Wheeler reined in his mount and listened intently to the sound of gunfire in the distance. He immediately skirted around to the east away from the settlement, keeping out of sight behind a rocky escarpment, hoping to find a safe way of reaching the besieged townsfolk. Half a mile further on, the grey suddenly gave a nervous whinny and came to a halt, pawing the ground. A hundred yards ahead the rocky terrain jutted out to prevent him from seeing what lay ahead. He slipped the Winchester out of its sheath as he dismounted. When he peeked around the rocky outcrop his eyes immediately fell on a naked figure staked out over a war-lance which had been buried in the earth. The point had finally worked its way through the victim's body. Knowing he could do nothing for him, he swiftly returned to his horse.

It took him the best part of an hour to reach his objective. From flat on his stomach on the rim of a hill overlooking the settlement he was able to observe what was happening down below. The wooden and adobe homes beyond the sparkling waters of the stream were charred ruins and piles of ashes. A thin, black cloud hovered menacingly over the settlement. 'Well at least they had enough sense to hole up in the church,' he said softly to himself, nodding in satisfaction at how they had organized their defences.

As he lay flat on his belly, taking it all in, trying to decide what to do for the best, the savages suddenly renewed their attack. The loud crack of gunfire coupled with their excited whooping cries reverberated eerily across the land towards him. He knew he was powerless to act for, had he tried to ride to their aid, the Apaches would have cut him down long before he could reach the church. There was nothing else for it but to sit tight, keep out of sight and adopt the role of interested observer.

He saw the smoke from the defenders' guns in the tower and at the windows as they returned fire. The Apaches did exactly as he expected, they drew fire, they probed for weaknesses and then they withdrew out of range. They lost only one warrior and two horses during the five-minute raid, which was a small price to pay for all the valuable ammunition the besieged townsfolk were forced to use up.

The pattern was repeated several times between late-afternoon and sunset. Only when the sun had dipped below the horizon and twilight began to settle upon the land did the Apaches call a halt to their sporadic, lightning raids. It wasn't long before their camp-fires lit up the darkening sky. Soon the incessant, rhythmic beating of their drums started to echo across the still land.

It was then that Wheeler made his move. He clambered slowly to his feet, flexed his aching side and then strolled leisurely back to his waiting horse. A quarter-moon appeared to share the cloudless sky with a myriad of twinkling stars, as he drew his pistol and urged his mount on at an easy gait up and over the brow of the hill.

The drums continued their spine-tingling cadence as he carefully picked his way down the steep slope, remaining vigilant every step of the way. He welcomed the sound, for he knew it might help to mask his approach. From the base of the hill he was able to make out the church silhouetted in the light of the calico moon and shimmering stars, 200 yards distant. His scheme was fraught with danger: if the uneven ground caused his horse to stumble, if the Apaches sensed his presence and cut him off from the church, or if the defenders inside the stone walls either fired on him or didn't open the doors quickly enough to admit him, he would be a dead man. He let such negative thoughts wash over him as he scanned the darkness one last time. Nothing stirred between him and the white walls. All he could make out was the flickering flames of the Apache camp-fires beyond the stream. There was nothing for it but to ride like the wind and put his faith in the Almighty. Pulling his hat down tight, like rough riders did when they were about to tackle a cranky horse, he kicked the grey into a flat-out gallop.

The Apache sentries heard him coming. A volley of rifle fire greeted the pounding of his horse's hooves as he tore on towards the church. Thinking the unseen rider was set on attacking them, two rifles also opened up from inside the church. Fortunately for Wheeler, none of the blind shots came close to hitting him. However, as he swung around the side of the church his luck finally ran out.

Twenty yards from safety the grey put his foot in an old gopher hole. The leg snapped with a sound like thunder as the horse collapsed from under him. Wheeler rolled over in the dirt until he came to a sudden, painful halt when his back struck a large boulder. The sound of approaching horses brought the shocked and winded scout to his feet. Ignoring the pain in his back and side he ran to his fallen horse, drew his Green River knife from his belt and quickly slit the animal's throat to end its suffering. He then grabbed his Winchester and spare ammunition from the saddle-bags and set off at break-neck speed for the church as bullets whistled and pinged all about him.

Somehow, more by luck than judgement, he managed to reach the front of the church unscathed. He pounded urgently on the battle-scared doors screaming, 'Open the God-damned doors!'

'Who's there?' demanded an animated voice from inside.

'Ty Wheeler!' The doors were immediately pulled open to admit

166

him. 'I thought for a minute y'all was intent on leavin' me out there,' he said, stepping inside. The doors were quickly slammed shut behind him. Everywhere the scout looked he saw tired, scared faces. 'How y'all doin'?' he asked, as Carlson came wearily across the floor to greet him.

'Not good,' advised the Swede, with a sad shake of his head. 'We have already lost three good men.'

'How are y'all fixed for ammunition?'

Carlson shrugged his shoulders. 'I've about twenty rounds left. I don't know about the others.'

'Well, don't go wasting any,' the scout advised, 'you'll be needing every last round before this little shindig's over.'

'Vot are our chances?' asked the store-keeper, lowering his voice a shade so as not to be overheard by the women and children at the far end of the church.

'Well, the walls are thick,' revealed

Wheeler, 'and that's a point in our favour.'

'Can we expect any help from the army, Mr Wheeler?' asked Father O'Farrell, as he joined them by the door.

'Maybe,' replied the scout. 'I sent my sister's boy to Joe Brady's place. With luck he could have a patrol here by mid-morning.'

'So what do we do for now?' asked Jed Gessner.

Wheeler explained in concise terms what needed to be done. 'Those not on watch should try and catch some sleep, they're gonna need it,' he advised at the end of his lecture.

'How can anyone sleep with that infernal row going on outside?' argued Jed Gessner, referring to the monotonous beat of the drums emanating from across the stream.

'Well, I for one can just about sleep through anything when I've a mind to,' replied Wheeler, with a wry grin. Without further ado he shouldered his

Winchester and wandered off in search of a comfortable spot where he could stretch out for a few hours. 'Make sure one of you wakes me before dawn,' he called back over his shoulder.

Tom Gessner nodded. 'I'll wake you, Mr Wheeler,' he promised.

He found leg room over by the women and children. Having tipped his hat to the ladies, he settled himself down on the stone floor. The wound in his side and the bruises on his back ached like the devil, but he tried to ignore his discomfort. He glanced up at the numerous torches burning around the walls. They cast a macabre glow about the stuffy, subdued room, producing just enough flickering light to reflect the fear in the faces of the women and children huddled up together on the floor. He knew they would all have good reason to feel afraid come morning.

15

Young Johnny Gates resisted the temptation to press on too quickly across the rugged land between his father's ranch and Joe Brady's enormous spread along the Gila River. He might have been tender in years but he had a sound knowledge of the land and an acute awareness of its many pitfalls. This, together with an abundance of common sense, enabled him to face his rather daunting ride with an air of justifiable confidence.

The sun was sinking low when he entered a wide sandy plain dotted with cactus, sagebrush, clumps of chaparral and short grass. From his elevated position he could just make out in the distance a meandering river whose waters fairly sparkled in the late evening sunshine.

'That must be the Gila, gal,' he

said excitedly, patting the sorrel's neck affectionately. He eased the mare gently into motion down the long easy gradient towards the valley below.

It was twilight by the time he reached the banks of the river. A quarter-moon was slowly ascending into the heavens as if to supervise the passage of the countless twinkling stars that were already dancing their way across the darkening sky. He followed the river, feeling pretty smug that he had made it so far without once losing his way. From what his uncle had said, he figured he still had about a two-hour ride ahead of him. But, as long as he kept the river in sight, he knew he wouldn't have any problem in locating the Brady ranch, no matter how dark it got.

They had travelled about a mile when his horse suddenly gave a nervous snort and came to an abrupt halt on the river-bank. 'What's got you all spooked, gal?' he asked softly. Night was rapidly spreading its dark cloak across the uncomfortably warm land, turning the friendly nopal and chaparral into grotesque, threatening shapes that set the boy's heart racing. When a lone coyote suddenly howled at the rising moon from the other side of the river, he just about jumped out of his skin. He slipped out of the saddle and stood beside his mount. When the sorrel lifted its head and snorted, he placed a hand over its flaring nostrils to keep her quiet.

He was more than half-convinced that the coyote call came from an Apache who had designs on his scalp. 'Apaches don't attack at night,' he whispered to himself in hesitant fashion. Then he remembered what his Uncle Ty was forever telling him during his infrequent visits to the ranch, never take anything for granted with the Apache, for they'll always do what you least expect! He had little choice but to go on. After a momentary hesitation he led the sorrel forward at the walk, his heart beating at a rapid rate.

He had covered a distance of about fifty yards when he stumbled over an object lying in his path. It gave him quite a shock. 'What the hell?' he complained irritably. When he probed the obstacle with his foot, he discovered to his horror that it was a body. As a scream formed in his throat a dark shape suddenly loomed up behind him to clamp a rough, sweaty hand over his mouth and a powerful arm around his heaving chest.

Johnny fought for all he was worth, but the more he struggled the tighter his captor's grip became. He didn't give up. Without a second thought he stamped down hard on his foe's foot and then followed up by running his boot down his other leg.

'Will you quit kicking me, kid, before I knock you on the head!' his assailant whispered gruffly into his ear. Johnny instantly ceased struggling. He stood still, his heart beating at twenty to the dozen, a curious frown forming on his troubled brow. His mind quickly registered the fact that the person holding him was no Apache. He spoke with a grizzled, western drawl and stank of chewing tobacco, cheap whiskey and horses. The hand covering his mouth fell away but not the armlock around his chest. He trembled a little and then tried to compose himself.

'Who are you, mister?' he asked, keeping his voice low.

'Shush,' whispered his companion, putting a finger to his lips. 'I'll tell you when we get outa here. The Apaches who killed the cowhand are still around,' he revealed. 'But don't fret none, youngun, I'll see you all reet.' He released his hold on him. 'My horse is back yonder a piece,' he advised, pointing over his shoulder away from the shallow, rippling waters of the river. 'Mount up and follow me, nice and easy. At the first sign of trouble lit a shuck away from the river and I'll find you when it's safe.'

'What if you can't find me?' replied

Johnny, waving away the man's rancid breath.

'Don't be afeared, bub,' he said, with a broad grin, 'I could find you blindfold.'

Johnny nodded hesitantly. 'All right,' he agreed. Doing his best to stay as quiet as a church mouse, Johnny allowed his companion to boost him up on to the sorrel. The man then took hold of the reins and led the way slowly to the spot where he had left his own horse.

'We'll ride for Joe Brady's place,' said the man, hauling himself up into the saddle.

'Good,' said Johnny, 'that's where I was heading when you found me.'

'You can tell me all about it once we're in the clear,' said his companion, as he came abreast of him. 'Stay close, bub,' he advised, setting off at a trot.

It was close to midnight by the time they reached the Brady ranch. Both the main house and the bunkhouse were in darkness when they rode in, but the sound of their approach soon drew a light. 'Who goes there?' demanded a loud voice from the open doorway of the bunkhouse. The man held a coal-oil lamp in his left hand and a gun in his right. 'Speak up or get yer heads blowed off!'

'Take it easy, pard,' cried Johnny's companion, as they reined in. 'We're friends.'

'That's what you say!' exclaimed the ranch hand.

'What in tarnation's a'goin' on here?' cried another excited voice from the doorway of the main house. A tall, powerfully built figure stood silhouetted in the dim yellow light emanating from the house.

'That's just what I'm a trying to find out, Mr Brady,' said the ranch hand. 'State your business, mister.'

'My name's Jake Parkes,' answered the man at Johnny's side. 'And I scout for the army. I've been trailing a bunch of Apaches for most of the day.'

'Horseshit!' interrupted the impatient

young cowhand, stepping forward a pace to confront the riders. 'The cavalry from the fort stopped by late this afternoon. They told us they was chasing a few of Geronimo's bucks back across the border a ways south of here. Ain't no more Apach' round these parts.'

'You couldn't be more wrong,' corrected Parkes.

'OK, Pete, I'll handle this,' said Joe Brady, stepping forward to confront his unexpected visitors. He stretched up his hand to the scout. 'I'm Joe Brady, this is my spread. What can we do for you?'

'Never mind all that,' interrupted an animated Johnny, impatiently. He had grown tired of all the pointless jawing and postulating and had decided to bring matters to a head. 'My folks and the people over at Medicine Bow need help, and they need it now!'

'Mind your manners, boy, I'm a speaking to Mr Parkes reet now, so hush up.'

'I will not!' argued Johnny defiantly. 'A lot of folks are in trouble, you gotta listen to me.'

'Do I know you, boy?' demanded Brady tetchily, peering at him quizzically through the gloom. He was of a mind to yank the sassy kid right off his horse and leather his hide good.

'You sold my pa the sorrel I'm a'riding last spring.'

'Are you Tod Gates's boy?' asked Brady. Johnny nodded. 'I think you'd all best come on in the house while we talk some,' he suggested. He led them into the house and invited them to sit at the table in the middle of the room. 'Now why don't you tell me what's goin' on?' he said. 'I've a feeling your tale's gonna be a mite interestin'!'

16

Just as Wheeler had predicted, the Apaches hit them again at first light. They came with a sudden rush, blood-curdling yells echoing unnervingly off the walls. 'Here they come!' yelled Jed Gessner from his position high above the floor by one of the openings in the west wall. A haunting, guttural scream died on his lips when a feathered shaft appeared, as if by magic, in his throat. He toppled over backwards to land on the solid floor, taking the stacked pews with him.

A woman screamed in fear as snarling, painted faces appeared in several of the openings. Wheeler's Winchester barked twice in rapid succession to account for the first of the savages. Others immediately appeared in the openings to take their place.

From their vantage point in the tower, Carlson and Potts cursed at their inability to draw a bead on the attackers who had their backs pressed right up against the walls of the church. 'I can't see 'em!' exclaimed Potts.

'Stay here,' roared Carlson, 'I'm going below to help.'

The Swede rushed to the stairs and descended them as quickly as his massive frame would allow. The acrid stench of spent cartridges and sweaty bodies assailed his nostrils as he reached ground level. His eyes quickly darted back and forth through the smoky haze, trying to make sense of the chaotic scene that confronted him. The horses inside the building were whinnying and prancing around in fear. He caught sight of a young Apache who was about to leap on the back of Hal Lines, who was struggling hand to hand with another buck. Carlson snapped his heavy rifle to his shoulder and pulled the trigger. The Apache in the opening gave a muffled grunt and toppled forward head first into the sniper's nest erected by the opening. The Indian and the entire structure crashed down right on top of Hal Lines and the buck he was grappling with. The three of them ended up in a still, crumpled heap on the floor, buried beneath the pews.

'Watch the windows!' yelled Wheeler, as the blade of his knife clashed with a metallic ring against that of the short, thin Apache who was circling him. Carlson did just that as Wheeler fought to keep the Indian at bay. Time and again the Apache thrust his blade forward in an underhand loop, seeking to drive it up into the scout's ribs, but each time Wheeler managed to deftly counter each movement. Eventually, the Apache's patience ran out. He sprang at the scout like a big cat. They toppled backwards to wrestle for position on the floor, each trying to get a grip on the other's knife hand. Just when Wheeler thought he was gaining the upper hand, the Apache managed to get his knife through his defences. He cried out in pain and fury when the tip of the wicked blade sliced through his side to reopen his old wound. Then, quite unexpectedly, the Indian gave a loud grunt and fell away limply to the side. When Wheeler looked up he saw Father O'Farrell standing over him. The barrel of the gun in the priest's hand was still smoking.

'I figured you might be wanting a hand, Mr Wheeler,' he said calmly, letting the hand holding the pistol fall to his side. He promptly offered his other hand to the scout.

Wheeler gratefully accepted the padre's hand up. 'Thank you, Father,' he replied, as his eyes swept the room. 'Now I know what they mean by the hand of God!'

'I think we've driven them off,' said the padre, glancing up at the empty windows.

'They'll be back,' insisted Wheeler, looking down at the blood flowing from his side. 'Galdarn it! Begging your pardon, Padre,' he added hastily. 'Same darned spot as got nicked before.'

'I'm sure one of the women will see you right,' suggested O'Farrell. Before Wheeler could reply, Carlson arrived on the scene.

'Are you OK?' asked the Swede, looking a trifle concerned.

'Yeah,' replied the scout. 'I'll live.'

'We lost Jed Gessner killed, and Hal Lines is also hurt pretty bad. Do you think we can hold them off if they charge again?'

Wheeler shrugged his shoulders. 'Maybe,' he said. 'But we sure can't afford to lose any more men.'

'What will they do to the women and children if they do manage to break in?' asked the padre.

'If that happens, Padre,' replied Wheeler, 'someone has to make sure they don't get taken alive!'

Before they could continue their conversation they were interrupted by the loud, insistent voice of Ben Potts hollering down from the tower. 'Here they come again!' he yelled. 'Still plenty enough to go around.'

The attack lasted but a few minutes, during which time the hard-pressed defenders suffered no further casualties. When the Apaches had withdrawn back across the stream, the padre had Ben Potts's wife clean and patch Wheeler's wound. She was forced to use a long strip of material torn from her young daughter's cotton petticoat for a bandage. 'You really need it restitching,' she told him. 'But this'll hold you for now.' He thanked her for her kindness as he accepted a canteen of water from the padre. Having quenched his thirst, he handed the canteen back to O'Farrell and then left to check on the men in the tower.

Potts and Carlson were keeping a watchful eye on the Apaches. 'Them stinkin' heathens is up to sommit,' advised Potts, as Wheeler placed a friendly hand on the look-out's tired shoulder and gazed past him at the activity across the stream.

'How many bullets y'all got left?' enquired the scout.

'Ten for my Henry and six more for my Navy Colt,' replied Potts.

'And I have six,' sighed Carlson, 'counting the one already in the breech of my rifle. What about you?'

'Fifteen rounds between my Winchester and pistol,' said Wheeler, removing his hand from Potts's shoulder.

'What the hell are they a'doin' over there with that wagon?' asked Potts, craning his neck for a better view.

'I reckon they're gonna set it on fire and ram the doors,' said Wheeler. 'I knew they'd get around to it sooner or later. Let's go down below, we can't do much good up here no more.' The three men trooped down to join the others. Carlson wrinkled his nose in disgust at the overpowering stench of horse dung, urine and burnt powder that wafted up to meet them. For some reason his companions didn't seem to notice, or maybe they were past caring about such trivialities.

Wheeler set about organizing their last stand. First, the men moved the horses to the very back of the building out of harm's way. Next, he whispered a reminder into the padre's ear about taking care of the women and children if and when the time came. Finally, he ordered the men and older children to realign the pews into a defensive barricade across the centre of the room. When the task had been completed to his satisfaction, the defenders took up position behind the barricade. A strange, eerie silence descended upon the church. No one spoke. Even the horses remained still and quiet. It was as if they all imagined they could hide in the silence. The padre bowed his head and prayed for a miracle. But, when a moment later he heard the awful, whooping of their tormentors and the thundering of horses' hooves, he knew with a stone-cold certainty that his prayers had not been answered. He lifted his head and nodded sadly at Davy Lines and Lance Potts, the two

186

teenage boys whom he knew Carlson had entrusted with the task of putting a bullet through every woman and child when things got desperate. They had been glad to learn that the padre would share their awful burden. He had also promised to kill them both if they ran out of ammunition before they could turn their guns on themselves.

The war cries and the almost deafening pounding of charging horses grew more intense with each passing second. Then, above the general clamour of the attacking hordes, the defenders heard an altogether different sound. The burning wagon came rolling, bouncing and crackling towards the front of the building. Instinctively they ducked their heads down and braced themselves for the impact. Suddenly the whole building seemed to shake right down to its very foundations as the fiery battering ram smashed into the robust doors with a loud, splintering crash.

The stone slabs beneath his feet were

still vibrating when Wheeler raised his head to inspect the damage. He was amazed to see that although the doors had buckled under the impact they were stubbornly refusing to give way completely. But the fierce crackling of the flames eating away at the dry timbers suggested that their reprieve would be short lived. 'Get ready,' he yelled above the excited noise emanating from the other side of the walls, 'they'll charge the second the fire burns through.'

It wasn't long before the flames started to lick their way through the top of the doors. They could smell the charred wood and feel the intense heat generated by the fire. Some of the younger children started to cry. 'Quit your squawking,' yelled Tom Gessner in response to the cacophony of wailing and screaming. 'It's worse than listening to them devils outside.' But his angry words had no effect on the terrified kids.

'Take it easy, Tom,' said Ben Potts,

laying a hand on the youth's trembling shoulder. 'We're all afraid, but there ain't no call to take it out on the kids.'

Before Tom Gessner could tell him to go to hell, a long, creaking, groaning sound heralded the moment they had all been dreading. With a mighty crash the doors collapsed inwards, throwing up a scorching hot curtain of crackling, spitting flames that prevented the eager Apaches from gaining immediate entry to the building.

As the flames began to die down the padre crossed himself and then looked forlornly towards the women and children. He knew that within a matter of minutes he would have to carry out his promise to Wheeler. Between him and his two teenage assistants they had exactly the right number of bullets to get the job done.

'Come on you red heathens!' screamed Tom Gessner. 'Let's get to it.'

As if in answer to his challenge a young Apache suddenly charged recklessly through a narrow gap in the receding flames to hurl a feathered war lance at the barricade. It thudded harmlessly into an overturned pew a foot away from Gessner's head. Wheeler's gun cut the buck down as he reached for his knife. The other warriors gathered just outside the building responded with a withering volley of arrows and bullets which splintered the wooden barricade in a dozen places.

Wheeler knew that the end was near. The Apaches would soon be able to rush them. He lifted the Winchester to his shoulder once more and took careful aim at the doorway, intent on killing as many as possible before they got to him. A tall, thin Apache wearing the shirt of a Mexican peon appeared before him. As he took careful aim at the prancing warrior, he suddenly heard the sound of heavy gunfire erupting all around the church. The snarling Apache gave a high-pitched scream and pitched forward on to his face into the dying flames. A puzzled frown formed on the scout's face. Then, through the smoke and haze, he saw the Apaches at the front of the building start to scatter and run in all directions. 'What the hell?' he said aloud to himself, as he rose from his position behind the barricade.

'Vot's happening?' demanded Carlson.

Wheeler scrambled awkwardly over the shoulderhigh barricade and crept forward stealthily to investigate the confused scene beyond the pock-marked walls of the church. A relieved smile quickly formed on his face when he caught sight of the Apaches in full-scale retreat. They were already a good hundred yards to the south of the church. A dozen or more riders were hot on their tail. 'It's OK,' he called back over his shoulder. 'It's all over, y'all can come on out now.'

As the others slowly and cautiously emerged from the smoky interior of the building, some blinking in response to the bright glare of the sun, others raising a hand to shield their eyes, he heard a horseman approaching. A broad grin spread rapidly across his face when the familiar figure of Jake Parkes reined in directly in front of him. 'I can't pretend that you ain't a sight for sore eyes,' he said, good-naturedly. Wheeler stretched up a hand to his friend, who shook it warmly. 'Who are your friends?'

'A bunch of Joe Brady's buckaroos. They kinda insisted on taggin' along.'

'How'd you know we needed help?'

'I happened across your young nephew last night, just as he was a figurin' on getting hisself parted from his hair,' he said. 'Ain't much of the settlement left,' he added, gazing towards the burnt-out ruins.

'Homes can be rebuilt.' insisted Wheeler. 'All it takes is the will to start over.'

'Johnny said Victorio was a-leadin' 'em.' Wheeler nodded in agreement. 'I seen another I recognized,' revealed Parkes, pausing for effect when his friend raised his eyebrows. 'Geronimo.'

'You sure?'

'I'm certain. Seen him back in '70 when Cochise signed the treaty. I'll never forget his ugly face in a hurry!' he said, as Brady's men circled up around them, throwing up a great cloud of dust.

'You must be Wheeler,' said Joe Brady, dismounting and extending his hand to the scout. He grunted in surprise and admiration at the vice-like grip that matched his own. 'Glad we made it in time.'

'Not half as glad as we are!' replied Wheeler, happily.

'Is there anything more me and my boys can do to help?'

'Yeah,' said Wheeler. 'If and when the cavalry show up tell 'em to come on fast. I'll try and leave 'em a clear trail to follow.'

'You're not going after them Apach'?'

'I sure am,' rejoined Wheeler. 'They've got some white kids with them. Probably ain't much I can do about it, but I'm sure gonna try. Now if'n the army is smart, there's a fair chance they can catch up to them before they cross over into Mexico. If they have any Apache scouts with them have the officer in charge send them on ahead at a fast lick.'

'All reet,' agreed Brady, 'I'll give them your message. Anything else?'

'Yeah, I need a mount and all the ammunition you can spare.'

The rancher turned to one of his cowhands. 'Give Wheeler your horse, Kyle,' he said. 'Collect whatever else you need from my men, and good hunting, my friend.'

Wheeler nodded his appreciation and moved swiftly away to gather up what he needed for his ride. When he was ready he turned to Parkes and said, 'Well, are you coming or ain't you?'

Parkes's yellow teeth flashed him a good-natured grin. 'Quit talkin' and lead the way,' he said. 'Time's a'wastin'.'

17

Less than an hour after Wheeler and
Parkes took off in pursuit of the
Apaches, a dusty, haggard-looking,
twenty-man cavalry patrol arrived at
the settlement. The drumming of their
horses' hooves, the musical tinkling of
their bridles and the metallic clinking of
army sabres announced their presence
to those sheltering in the cool of the
church.

There was a supercilious air about
the officer in charge. He sat astride
his mare surveying the expectant sea
of tired, dirty faces arrayed before him
as he toyed with his moustache, like a
proud peacock preening himself. It was
almost as if dealing with these ragged
people was beneath his dignity. Ben
Potts took an instant dislike to the
pretentious fool. He quietly wondered
if the officer was addicted to opium, for

he'd seen a similar glazed look in the eyes of a number of Chinese workers he had toiled beside on the railroad back in the late '60s.

When the padre gave a light, hesitant cough, the officer snapped out of his apparent trance. He dismounted in a quick, jerky fashion, muttering a complaint under his breath about the infernal heat. 'Who's in charge here?' he demanded, in an accent that was unmistakably well-bred English.

'Ain't no one rightly in charge,' replied Potts, blandly.

The officer ignored him and turned to face the padre. 'Are you people all right?'

'We're alive, praise be to God,' said Father O'Farrell. He too had taken an instant dislike to the man, for he reminded him of many similar self-opinionated Englishmen he had encountered back in his native Ireland.

'Guess you must be in charge of these here soldier boys,' observed Joe Brady, pushing his way through the hushed crowd. 'You got a name, fella?' he asked, sinking his hands deep into his pants pocket.

'I am Major Atkinson, 9th United States Cavalry, out of Fort Dobbs. And who might you be?'

'The name's Brady and I owns a spread down by the Gila River. Me and my boys got word that these good folks were in trouble, so we rode on over to lend them a hand. Some of my other hands are out scouring the territory for army patrols reet now.'

'We ran into your man Jepson at dawn this morning,' revealed Atkinson, eyeing the man warily. 'He told us these people might be in trouble, so we came as fast as we could. I'm just glad you decided to help out.'

'Me and mine ain't in the habit of turning a blind eye to those in need,' said the rancher, locking eyes with the patronizing major. 'Now I've a message for you if you care to listen.'

'A message?' snapped Atkinson. 'For me? From whom?'

'A scout, name of Wheeler,' replied Brady.

'Ty Wheeler?' The rancher merely nodded. 'He was here?' Brady nodded again irritably. The major slapped his gauntlets against his right thigh testily. 'What's the message?' he demanded tersely. Brady repeated the scout's message word for word. Atkinson then turned to face his adjutant, Captain Tisdale, and, making no attempt to conceal his fury, roared, 'Who the hell does this Wheeler think he is? Giving me orders, by thunder!'

'Wheeler seems to know his business,' interjected Ben Potts, feeling a need to speak up for the man who had been instrumental in his, and many others' survival. 'It might pay you soldier boys to do just what he says. He sure seems to know Apaches.'

'When I want your opinion, sir, I'll ask for it,' snapped Atkinson, pulling on his gauntlets.

'How long you been in Arizona,

Major?' asked Brady, his hackles rising by the second.

'Long enough,' retorted Atkinson sharply, turning his back on the rancher. Hastily he put a foot in the stirrup and hauled himself up into the saddle.

Brady stepped forward and swiftly grabbed hold of the bridle of the major's horse. 'I ain't sure whether you're an arrogant fool or just a darned blasted ignorant one, but either way, mister, you better start treading soft around me. I don't hold with none of your old-fashioned English etiquette. Rile me again and I'll come at you every which way I can!'

'Let go of my bridle, Mr Brady,' hissed Atkinson menacingly, 'or I'll have you clapped in irons for obstructing an officer of the government.'

'I'd love to see you try,' sneered the rancher, as several of his riders drew their guns and levelled them at the nervous-looking soldiers. Atkinson glanced about anxiously for support from his troopers, but none was forthcoming. Brady's cowhands had the drop on them and they knew it.

Atkinson's face turned puce with rage. He glared down at the poker-faced rancher and growled, 'I'll not forget this, Mr Brady. I am not a man to be trifled with.'

'Nor am I,' promised the rancher, letting go of the bridle and stepping clear.

Atkinson swung about to address his second-in-command. 'Have the men water their horses at the stream. We'll give the company surgeon time to deal with the civilian casualties.'

'And then will we return to the fort, sir?' asked Tisdale.

'No!' snapped Atkinson. 'We're going after that blasted scout!'

18

For the rest of the day, Wheeler and Parkes stubbornly pursued the fleeing Apaches as they melted away, first east and then south, towards the Mexican border and the comparative safety of the Sierra Madre Mountains. The raiders made no attempt to cover their tracks, even though they must have suspected that the soldiers would follow them. Speed was their main priority, for they knew that once they reached the rugged mountains that straddled the border they would be able to evade capture indefinitely in the maze of narrow canyons and precipitous rocky passes that they knew so well.

They were in good heart, for they were loaded down with scalps and other booty looted from the various ranches they had raided. They drove before them a large herd of horses which they planned to trade for food, whiskey and guns to unscrupulous businessmen below the border. Their two child captives would also fetch a handsome price on the thriving slave market, which the Mexican Government conveniently turned a blind eye.

Hour after hour, the scouts kept up their relentless, gritty pursuit of the hostiles, pausing only to rest their lathered mounts, or snatch a drink of tepid water from their canteens. All the while the unforgiving sun beat down upon their heads with a savage intensity, draining their energy, drenching them in sweat and testing their resolve to keep going. But giving up wasn't an option, nothing was going to stop them riding down their quarry.

Late in the afternoon, the parched grassy plain they were traversing gave way to a wide, sandy, broken expanse of saguaro and tumbleweed-covered jornado. The landscape was dotted with rugged, reddish-brown, rocky buttes that jutted up towards the sky like silent sentinels standing guard over the desert. Wheeler reached for the canteen tied around his saddlehorn. He gave it a quick shake and discovered it to be half-full. 'How you doing for water?' he asked his companion, taking a quick swill from his own canteen.

'Got about five good swallows left,' replied Parkes, stretching cramp-knotted muscles. 'Enough to keep me going for a while yet.'

'Them Apach' are settin' one helluva pace,' observed Wheeler. 'I reckon we've fallen a good two hours behind them.'

'You wanna press on a mite and close the gap?'

'No, not until those soldier boys catch up to us.'

'That's if'n they're a'comin'.'

'Yeah,' sighed Wheeler. 'That thought's been bugging me too.'

Close to sunset they came across a water-hole in the shadow of a sheer-sided rocky outcrop on the far side of the desert. But the discovery brought them no joy, for the Apaches had poisoned the water by bleeding a pony to death in the centre of the basin. The two friends stared long and hard at the bloody carcass in silent frustration. 'Never miss a God damned trick, do they?' complained Parkes, venting his anger on a loose rock by kicking it violently into the crimson coloured water with the toe of his boot. It disappeared with a loud splash.

'Let's pitch camp,' suggested Wheeler, 'it'll be dark soon. We'll snatch a few hours' sleep and make an early start come morning.'

'Sure thing,' agreed Parkes. 'If'n them soldier boys is a-comin' to help us, it'll give them a chance to catch up to us.'

A good two hours before dawn, while the stars still shone brightly out of the inky-blue canopy overhead, the two scouts were back in the saddle. They picked up the Apaches' trail on the far side of the rocky cliffs and followed it south across a high, undulating, sparsely grassed plateau littered with shallow, dry washes, giant boulders, tall cacti and scattered clumps of chaparral. All the while their eyes keenly scanned the wild, ravine-scarred country for any sign of ambush.

An hour after first light they came across their quarry's overnight campsite. They examined the ashes of their cooking fires and found the bones of the pony they had slaughtered for their evening meal. Parkes also discovered the tracks of five new riders who had joined the main band sometime during the night. 'Lookee here, pard,' he said, drawing his companion's attention to the sign. 'Geronimo's got hisself some new recruits.'

'Ain't no surprise in that,' observed Wheeler, as he looked down at the tracks. 'My guess is that a lot more will slip away from the reservations to join him unless we can catch him first.'

'These five are from the band that fled the massacre,' said Parkes, rising from his squatting position in the dirt.

'How can you be sure?'

'D'you notice that shod print?' Wheeler nodded at the distinctive track his friend was pointing at. 'That hoss is the one they stole from the Brady spread when they bushwhacked his rider.'

'Then as long as the army catches up to us we can deal with all our bad eggs together,' said Wheeler. 'Come on, they ain't more than an hour or so ahead of us, let's ride.'

They continued south at a steady gait throughout the sultry morning, slowly but surely closing the gap on the hostiles. The light breeze blowing up from Sonora brought little relief from the blistering heat, but at least they found fresh water. Around midmorning they crossed a small, shallow, rippling stream where they paused to water their horses and fill their canteens before pressing on.

By noon they were fast approaching the foothills which led up into the rugged Dragoon Mountains. The granite peaks rose up in the distance, warning them that time was rapidly running out if they were to prevent the hostiles from making good their escape. It was then that Wheeler glanced back over his shoulder and noticed a rising cloud of dust just a couple of miles behind them. 'Reckon we might have help coming,' he said.

'Not before time,' replied Parkes, rotating his stiff neck.

'We'll wait for them to catch up,' said Wheeler, easing himself out of the saddle to stretch his legs. Parkes nodded and did likewise. They led their mounts to the side of the trail where they sheltered from the glare of the sun under the branches of a lone cottonwood tree.

Twenty minutes later, the clattering of horses' hooves on the hard ground heralded the arrival of the patrol. As Wheeler pushed his back away from the trunk of the tree and came forward to greet the soldiers, he suddenly sensed a presence close by. The horses tethered by the tree pricked up their ears and snorted in unison. It told him that they had caught the scent of an Apache on the breeze. His gun cleared leather in a flash, his eyes darting left and right, trying to locate the Apaches who had almost succeeded in sneaking up on them unnoticed. Parkes moved swiftly to his horse and pulled his carbine clear of the saddle. He chambered a fresh round and moved forward to support his friend. As he drew up alongside him a frightened young voice called out to them in Spanish from the rocks thirty yards off to their left. 'No shoot, no shoot! I come alone and in peace.'

Both men turned to face the Apache youth as he emerged from cover. 'Who are you?' demanded Wheeler in Spanish.

'I am Nayasile,' replied the youth. He came forward slowly with his hands raised high in the air before him to demonstrate that he carried no weapons. 'I am with those who escaped from Porico's camp.'

'You was ridin' with Geronimo?' enquired Wheeler, keeping his gun levelled on the boy. The Apache nodded.

'Yes,' replied the youth. 'My people joined them this morning, after two days of searching. But they are foolish. Only death awaits those who follow Geronimo. The long knives are coming, they will kill all.' The patrol galloped into sight as the boy spoke. Wheeler ignored them as he continued to focus his attention on the youth.

'Where are the rest?' he asked, calmly.

'In the hills,' replied Nayasile.

'What's going on here?' demanded a haughty voice from the rear. Atkinson, his face bright pink from too many hours in the sun, strode up to join the two scouts. 'Arrest that Indian. If he resists, shoot him.'

'Just hold fire a gall dang minute, Major,' retorted Wheeler. 'If'n you'll let me finish talking to him we might get some valuable intelligence.' Without waiting for a reply he swung back to face Nayasile. 'How do we know we can trust you?'

'I bring present,' replied the boy, casting a wary eye about him.

'What's he saying?' snapped Atkinson, impatiently.

'He says he comes in peace,' replied Wheeler. 'He also says he's brung us a gift.' The scout turned back to face the boy. 'What's this present you speak of?'

'Look to the ponies in the rocks,' he replied, pointing towards the spot from which he had emerged from cover.

Wheeler told Parkes to keep him covered. Ignoring a further protest from the major, he strode off towards the tall boulders and promptly disappeared from sight. He was back within minutes leading an old palomino pony on whose back sat two dirty, ragged, tearey-eyed white children.

'Well I'll be,' said Parkes. 'He's brung the kids back to us.'

'Mr Wheeler,' growled Atkinson, 'will you be good enough to tell me just what the hell is going on here? Who are these children?'

Wheeler halted the pony directly in front of the major and lifted the children gently down to the ground. He ruffled the boy's matted hair and gave him and his sister a reassuring smile. 'The kids are from a relay station near Medicine Bow,' he advised. 'Geronimo killed their folks. The Apache boy managed to sneak them back to us.'

'Why?' Atkinson demanded arrogantly. 'Why would an Apache want to help us?'

Wheeler shrugged his shoulders.

'Did he say where the hostiles are?' pressed Atkinson impatiently.

'They'll be lying in wait somewhere up ahead,' advised Wheeler. 'There's a hundred likely spots for an ambush, so we'd best be careful if we're going after them.'

'Thanks for the advice, Wheeler,' said the major, with an air of sarcasm.

'But I think we can manage without your help from here on in.'

'Suit yourself,' replied the scout, casting an eye over the assembled ranks of broody, dusty troopers. Most of them were experienced men who had fought the Apache before, but a few were green recruits who were likely to freeze at the vital moment. Quite a number of them had taken part in the massacre at Porico's camp. He nodded at Ned Forbes, the young scout the major had brought along as tracker. Ned was a pleasant, honest fellow, but one who still had a great deal to learn. Wheeler was somewhat surprised that he had been chosen over more experienced guides, including tame Apache scouts who had served the army well over a period of many years. 'You didn't bring any Apache scouts,' he observed, with an air of disappointment.

'Too right we didn't,' replied Atkinson. 'They're not to be trusted. And anyway, Ned Forbes has proved his worth. He followed your trail easy enough.'

'Ned's purty good,' agreed Wheeler, 'but he don't compare to an Apache when it comes tuh tracking. None of us do. We have a saying in Arizona, Major: it takes an Apache to find an Apache.'

'Meaning what, Wheeler?'

'Meaning that an Apache scout would be able to locate their hiding place real quick and save you from walking into an ambush.'

'So can Forbes,' insisted the major stubbornly. 'Go home, Wheeler, we don't need you or your opinions.' Atkinson turned his back on the angry scout and addressed Tisdale. 'I want that Indian tied to the back of a horse,' he instructed, nodding towards Nayasile. 'Have two of the troopers stay here to guard him and the children.'

'Are we going after the hostiles?' asked Tisdale.

'Yes!' snapped Atkinson. 'Forbes, take the lead. Let's move out.'

'That damn fool's gonna get them all killed,' muttered Wheeler.

'What d'you figure on doing?' asked Parkes.

'Get the company saw-bones to stitch me up again,' grumbled Wheeler. 'Then we'll go after them.'

'Somehow that's just what I figured we'd do,' grinned Parkes, as he moved off to attend to their horses.

19

By the time Wheeler's wound was attended to, the patrol was already advancing deep into the dangerous foothills of the imposing Dragoon Mountains, with a stone-faced, anxious Ned Forbes at its head. The clip-clopping of horses' hooves, the creaking of saddle leather and the clinking of army sabres echoed off the walls of the steep-sided gully to announce their coming. The silent, brooding troopers could tell from the young scout's demeanour that he was scared witless. He was in strange country performing a task that was a world away from the regular tasks he undertook around the fort, such as tracking down the occasional horse-thief. Flushing out a large band of renegades was a job for a more experienced and cool head. The soldiers knew it, Forbes himself knew it, the only one who seemed oblivious to the fact was the haughty major, who rode along stroking his moustache as if he was out on a Sunday afternoon picnic.

Although they all had no liking for Wheeler and his liberal thinking, to a man they would have felt safer if he had been riding with them. They remained in a constant state of alert as they rode on up the draw. Their great fear was that the stubborn major would lead them into a deadly trap. Frightened eyes constantly darted back and forth, searching the high rocky walls on either side of the trail for hidden snipers. When the draw eventually opened out into a broad stretch of high, sandy plateau, and the major halted their advance, they breathed a collective sigh of relief.

Atkinson sat straight backed at the head of the column, waiting impatiently for Ned Forbes to return from his advanced position ahead of the patrol. He arrived in a cloud of dust, reining in directly in front of the irritable major. 'Well, Forbes, any sign of the hostiles?' demanded Atkinson.

The troopers nearest to him couldn't help but notice how edgy the scout looked. He gave a curt nod, 'Yeah, Major. They followed the arroyo up yonder for a piece and then cut away towards the ravine on the far side. I'd say the tracks are less than an hour old.'

'Then we're closing on them!' exclaimed Atkinson, pounding his fist against his saddle.

'Wouldn't we be better off sending a rider back for Wheeler and Parkes?' asked Luke Tanner, the veteran sergeant of the troop. 'They knows Apaches a bit better than young Forbes here. Might save us from riding headlong into an ambush.' A general murmur of agreement rose from the ranks.

'No!' snapped Atkinson, his voice cracking like a whip through the still air. 'Forbes is quite capable of finding the hostiles.'

'Finding them ain't likely to be that hard,' interceded another of the troopers, with a sarcastic chuckle, 'but escaping with our hair might be!'

'Hold your tongue, Soldier!' roared Atkinson. 'I'll not tolerate such talk. And the next man who seeks to challenge my authority will find himself up on a charge.' Some of the unhappy troopers cursed the major under their breath, others shook their heads sadly, while the majority just looked away in disgust. Atkinson swung back to face the cringing figure of Ned Forbes. 'Go on ahead,' he barked. 'Scout out the ravine and report back.' Forbes nodded and then rode off reluctantly to do the major's bidding. A few seasoned troopers feared the youngster was riding to his death, for the narrow ravine promised to be a perfect spot for an ambush.

A cold chill ran down the scout's spine as he slowed his mount to a walk at the mouth of the steepsided canyon. His throat suddenly felt very dry as he stared down at the confused jumble of tracks in the sand. He didn't want to go on, yet he knew he had to. The sound of his horse's hooves striking the loose rocks underfoot echoed eerily off the cliffs. He had never felt so alone in his entire life. On he rode, deeper into the canyon, up the slight gradient that led towards the mountains.

Fifty yards on he encountered a sharp right-hand bend in the trail. Having glanced up at the rocks all around, he gently eased his horse forward at the walk. Goose pimples formed on his bare arms, in spite of the heat of the day. All the while he wondered when he would hear the tell-tale swish of an arrow through the still, hot air or the crack of a rifle shot. But it didn't happen. When he finally reached the far end of the canyon without incident, he paused briefly to still his rapidly beating heart. He removed his hat, wiped the sweat from his brow and then started off back down the trail, convinced that all was well. There would be no Apache ambush here.

Had he been a little more experienced he would have recognized the clear warning signs all about him. But he was young and careless, which was why he failed to appreciate the significance of the total silence which enveloped him. He should have asked himself why no birds flew overhead or why no critters scurried this way and that amongst the rocks at the sound of his approach. His inexperience was to cost many a good man his life.

He found the patrol waiting for him at the mouth of the canyon. 'Well, Mr Forbes?' enquired Atkinson, raising his eyebrows. 'What did you find?'

Forbes smiled reassuringly and said, 'It's safe to go on, Major, the canyon's all clear. The Apaches musta rode on up into the mountains.'

'Then we'll advance,' decreed the major, turning to nod curtly at Tisdale. 'Have the men form up by twos, Captain.'

Tisdale raised his eyes to the jagged, inhospitable rocky wall that rose imperiously before him. Half a lifetime spent on the frontier had taught him to recognize a potential trap when he saw one. Despite the scout's happy assurances, he sensed danger. However, he lacked the necessary strength of character to register a protest, so he followed blindly on the tail of the glory-seeking major as he led the way forward.

Luke Tanner nervously fingered the butt of the army carbine protruding from the saddleboot at his knee. The nervous tension gnawing away at him caused the hairs on the back of his neck to stand on end. All his natural instincts told him they were riding into an ambush. One quick glance at the faces of the troopers following on behind him confirmed that they shared his sense of foreboding. Their eyes constantly darted back and forth in search of the enemy they all sensed was lying in wait for them. They were concentrating so hard on the rocky ledges and outcrops that they no longer even noticed the flies and other insects that accompanied them, or the intense heat.

They had almost reached the bend in the trail when Tanner suddenly heard the distinctive sound of a disturbed pebble clattering down the canyon wall to his left. Before he could cry out a warning, a volley of rifle fire exploded from the rocky ledges and boulders all about them. The horse of the trooper at his side whinnied in pain and fear and then toppled over on its side, spilling its rider into the dirt. As the surprised soldier jumped to his feet a bullet struck him between the eyes. He collapsed to the ground and lay still beside his horse. Two other troopers were downed before Tisdale's anguished scream was heard above the noise of the battle. 'Take cover!' he yelled. 'Shelter in the rocks, return fire.'

The majority of the milling troopers

panicked. Ignoring Tisdale's orders, they desperately tried to wheel their mounts about within the narrow confines of the gorge, hoping to gallop clear of the murderous crossfire. But all they succeeded in doing was making themselves easy targets for the Apache snipers high up in the rocks. Three more troopers were felled before another urgent appeal from Tisdale finally brought the men to their senses. They belatedly dived for cover amongst the boulders at the side of the trail as their terrified mounts galloped away from the noise and smoke of the battle. The few horses that stood their ground were quickly cut down by the Apaches.

From their sheltered positions above, behind and in front of the patrol, the Apaches were able to pick off their quarry without exposing themselves. The patrol was pinned down by the angry fire that pinged and whined off the rocks all about them. They snapped off the odd shot by way of reply, but quickly ducked back down the second they pulled the trigger. Hot lead continuously ricocheted dangerously about the floor of the canyon. The soldiers' position was desperate, and they knew it. It was only a question of time before the Apaches finished them off.

Atkinson sat motionless with his back tight up against a round boulder, sweat trickling down his temples, mumbling incomprehensibly to himself. Gone was the swagger and arrogance that characterized the way he normally dealt with people. In its place was a glazed look and trembling shoulders. Shock had set in. The gun in his hand had not even been cocked for action. He suddenly became aware of a hand on his shoulder and someone shouting, 'Major, Major!' into his ear. Looking up he gazed into the animated face of his adjutant. 'We have to do something!' yelled Tisdale, above the cacophony of gunfire.

'Huh?' queried Atkinson, as he came out of his dreamy state.

'Are you all right, sir?'

'Of course I am, Captain!' he snapped, regaining some measure of composure. He pulled back the hammer of his pistol and then took a deep breath. 'How many men have we lost?'

'Hard to say,' replied Tisdale, casting his eyes about the floor of the gorge. 'But one thing for sure, we're outgunned and in one hell of a mess. We're sitting ducks and unless we find a way out of here quickly, they'll kill us all.'

'What shall we do?'

Tisdale shook his head and then ducked down in response to a bullet which pinged against the top of the boulder they were cowering behind. 'I wish Wheeler was here, he'd know what to do.'

'Damn Wheeler!' roared the major. 'Damn all the scouts! It was one of them who led us into this trap in the first place. It's all that fool Forbes's doing. If we get out of here alive I'm going to have his head!'

'He's dead,' revealed Tisdale. 'I saw him fall.'

The major swung about and brought his pistol to bear on the rocks ahead of him. He fired blindly at where he imagined an Apache to be hiding. His shot brought a quick response from half-a-dozen rifles further up the trail. The bullets fizzed about him like a swarm of angry hornets, forcing him to keep his head down. Twenty feet away to his left he saw one of the troopers suddenly keel over in the sand and lie still. 'You got us into quite a pickle here, Major,' heckled Luke Tanner, from close-by. The sergeant paused to fire his Henry rifle at a puff of smoke he had seen materialize in a rocky cleft above his head and then said, 'What you planning to do about it?' The words were hardly out of his mouth when a bullet struck him in the leg, just above the boot. He cried out in pain, dropped his rifle and grabbed hold of his injured leg with both hands. In so doing he moved fractionally away from the rock that had been shielding his upper body. A second bullet instantly hit him between the shoulder blades. He grunted in surprise and pain before pitching forward on to his face in the dirt. His body went into spasm and then lay still as blood began to seep from the corner of his mouth.

Visibly shaken by what he had seen, the major whimpered in terror and tried to make himself as small as possible. He was convinced they were all going to die. In his frightened, confused state, he desperately tried to focus on all the things he had heard about the Apaches. The one thing which came to mind was the terrible torture they inflicted on live prisoners. He checked his gun. 'Must save the last shell for myself,' he whispered to himself. 'Mustn't let them take me alive.'

All about the floor of the canyon each of the scattered surviving troopers was facing the same deadly dilemma:

risk exposing themselves to return fire or stay hidden and allow the enemy to steadily close in for the kill? They all rapidly reached the same conclusion: it was better to go down fighting than merely sit tight and accept the inevitable. But for all their determined efforts not one Apache rifle was silenced.

Ten minutes into the battle six soldiers lay dead and five more were nursing debilitating wounds. The rest maintained their bitter resistance, but like their commanding officer a good many of them resolved to keep one bullet in reserve for when they were finally overrun.

Just when it seemed that the entire patrol was on the verge of annihilation, help arrived from an unexpected quarter. The hard-pressed troopers suddenly became aware of some frenzied activity in the rocks above their heads. At first they thought the Apaches were about to rush them, but then they realized that the warriors were responding to rifle fire at their backs. It had to mean that someone had managed to scale the craggy peaks and get behind the war party in order to fire down upon them. The Apaches were forced to vacate their positions, in so doing they exposed themselves to the guns of the soldiers down below.

The troopers couldn't believe their good fortune. For the first time since the battle started they were able to pick and choose their targets with impunity. Caught in a withering crossfire, the Apaches beat a hasty, ill-disciplined retreat. They darted in and out of the rocks like skittish mountain goats fleeing from a hungry cougar. Five never made it to safety. Two fell amongst the jagged rocks, three more plummeted down to land at the base of the cliffs. The rest of them melted swiftly away, firing as they went to dissuade the soldiers from following.

Tisdale was the first to show himself. He rose from cover, straightened his hat and then gazed up in wonder in the direction of the rocks, searching for the men who had come to the rescue of the patrol. With a happy glint in his eye, he strode forward, holstered his pistol and then looked back over his shoulder at the pathetic, quivering figure of his commanding officer who sat with his back propped up against a boulder. 'You can come out now, Major,' he said caustically, 'looks like it's all over.'

The major turned his head and stared up blankly at the captain. 'What about the Apaches?' he asked, nervously.

'They're all gone,' he advised. 'Someone drove them off.'

Atkinson came slowly to his feet. As he did so, two familiar figures appeared on a narrow rocky ledge to wave to the relieved troopers. A cheer went up from the ranks. Tisdale strolled forward to greet their saviours. 'I hope you soldier boys didn't mind us joining your little party?' said Wheeler, as he jumped down from a boulder to land directly in front of the captain.

'Thank God you did,' replied Tisdale, happily. Swiftly he removed his gauntlets and offered his hand to the scout. 'We're all mighty pleased to see you. We couldn't have lasted much longer.' They were instantly surrounded by a sea of happy faces. Several of the relieved troopers came forward to slap the newcomers on the back. Only Atkinson remained distant and aloof from proceedings, preferring to maintain a watching brief.

'How'd y'all manage to get up behind them Apach'?' asked one of the smiling troopers at Wheeler's shoulder.

'The Apache boy who returned the kids showed us the way,' advised Wheeler.

'I'll be damned!' exclaimed the trooper, scratching his head.

'I had me a little chat with him while the surgeon was fixing me up,' explained the scout. 'I managed to persuade him to tell me where Geronimo was figuring on snaring y'all. He agreed to show me how to get up behind them unseen.'

'Why?' demanded Atkinson high-handedly, stepping forward to confront the scout. 'Why did he help? What reason did he have?'

Wheeler shrugged his shoulders dismissively. 'Does it really matter why he helped?' he asked, making a bold effort to hold his temper in check. 'The fact is he did, so just be grateful.'

'Don't think for one moment it's going to make any difference to my plans to make an example of that little renegade,' growled the major, truculently. 'I intend to hang him when we return to the fort.'

'Well now, Major, you just might have a bit of problem there,' offered Wheeler, with a wry grin.

'And why would that be, Mr Wheeler?' queried Atkinson contemptuously.

'Well the kid kinda got away in the confusion of battle.'

'Got away! What you mean is you deliberately let my prisoner escape!'

Wheeler frowned. 'Now would I do a thing like that, Major?' A number of the troopers began to chortle amongst themselves. Not one of them doubted for a moment that Wheeler was guilty as charged. But even though they hated Apaches with a passion, none of them disapproved of the scout's action.

Atkinson was fit to be tied. He stood glaring at the scout for what seemed like an eternity, blind fury bubbling away within him. 'You meddled in army business, mister,' he snapped, stamping his foot on the ground like a spoilt child.

'Prove it!' replied Wheeler, defiantly.

'I don't have to,' insisted the major. 'Your actions over the past few days do that for me. Captain Tisdale, place this man under arrest.'

'I don't think I can do that, Major,' replied Tisdale.

'Why not?'

'He's a civilian.'

'So what?' roared Atkinson. 'He's aided and abetted in the escape of a military prisoner. That gives me grounds for ordering his detention.'

'He also saved the life of every man jack of us,' offered one of the troopers.

'I don't care,' screamed Atkinson, like a man possessed. 'Hold him!'

Wheeler sighed in exasperation. 'Major,' he said, stepping towards him, 'you are one dumb son-of-a-bitch.' Before the strutting, posturing officer could react, the scout smashed his right fist into the point of his jaw, pole-axing him to the ground.

'You shouldn't have done that, Wheeler,' remarked Tisdale, looking down at the unconscious figure at his side.

The scout shrugged his shoulders. 'So arrest me,' he said, his eyes daring the captain to try.

Tisdale swallowed hard and then caught the eye of two of the shocked troopers who were gaping openmouthed at their fallen commander. 'Pour some water on him,' he said, motioning towards Atkinson with his head. 'And then help him up.'

'The company surgeon and one of the two men you left to guard the kids are making their way down the far side of the cliff,' said Wheeler, as he turned away. 'They helped us hit the Apaches. I told them you'd meet them at the mouth of the canyon,' he advised.

'Wheeler,' called the captain. The scout turned to face him. 'Thanks.'

'Don't mention it, Captain,' replied Wheeler, touching his hat. With that he and Parkes walked slowly back down the gentle incline towards the mouth of the canyon and their waiting horses, leaving the troopers to bury the dead and tend to the wounded.

20

A silent, brooding Johnny Gates leaned against the inside front wall of the newly erected barn, watching his uncle saddle up. 'D'you have to leave today?' he pressed. 'Can't you stay for a while longer?'

Ty Wheeler swung around to face his nephew and smiled apologetically. 'You know I can't, Johnny,' he replied. 'I've got to get Chato over to San Carlos. We're already more than a week overdue. If'n we don't ride today, they'll be sending the army for him.'

' 'T'ain't fair!' he complained. 'You never stay long.'

'I've been here nigh on a month!' exclaimed his uncle, good-naturedly. 'I'd say that's a purty good visit.' He led his horse out into the bright morning sunshine to join Chato and the rest of his sister's family.

'Is he still giving you grief about leaving?' queried Tod Gates, as Wheeler and his son emerged from the barn.

Wheeler smiled and then ruffled the pouting youngster's hair. 'I'll say one thing about Johnny,' he offered, 'he don't give up easy.'

The two men shook hands briskly. 'Thanks again for all your help with the new barn. And don't be forgetting, my offer still holds; there'll always be a place for you here.'

'Thanks, Tod,' replied Wheeler, letting go of his brother-in-law's hand. 'I appreciate it, but I just ain't cut out to be a rancher.'

'We go now?' interjected a fully healed Chato, in slow, heavily-accented English.

'Hey, you savvy English purty good now, kid,' observed Wheeler.

'Johnny, good teacher,' observed the Apache, nodding towards the amused youngster. 'I try teach him Apache, but he not such a good learner!' They all laughed.

'OK,' said Wheeler, having given his sister a quick hug, 'let's ride.' With that the two of them set off at a canter in the direction of the Chiricahua reservation at San Carlos.

After a day and a half of hard riding, they forded a shallow stream and entered the bleak San Carlos reservation. Almost immediately they happened upon a small village of some ten wickiups. Within the camp a few old men were sitting around a stone circle drinking tiswin. In their befuddled state they never even noticed the riders as they passed by. On the far bank of the tiny stream that bisected the village, Wheeler caught sight of a number of forlorn-looking, emaciated Apaches who were valiantly trying to till the thin, infertile soil with the hopelessly inadequate tools supplied by the government. Things were even worse than he remembered from his previous visits. The other villages they skirted around on their way in were no better. It appeared from the dispirited expressions on their faces and the lethargy of their body language that the once proud Apaches were a broken people.

Right around noon they caught sight of the agency buildings through the shimmering heat. There was a ramshackle trading-post, a school and a rather drab-looking residence. A few curious Apache children observed their approach from the steps of the school through sullen, suspicious eyes. Wheeler reined in by the trading-post and nodded at his young charge to dismount. 'I no like this place,' said Chato, reverting to Spanish.

'You'll be fine once we get you settled with some of your own people,' insisted Wheeler. But his statement lacked real conviction. Part of him hated the idea of abandoning the boy to a future devoid of hope, but he had no choice. There was simply no place else for the kid to go. At least he would be comparatively safe amongst his own people, that's if he didn't starve to death. The two of them tethered their mounts to the hitching rail in front of the building, alongside three other horses, all of which carried army blankets and saddles.

At that precise moment the door in front of them swung open and two men stepped out into the bright sunshine. The first was a tall, thin, grey-haired cavalry officer who wore captain's epaulettes. His companion was a squat, beady-eyed figure.

'Who are yer?' demanded the man, tersely, halting directly in front of his visitors.

'The name's Wheeler. What's yourn?'

'Harry Maddocks, I'm the Indian agent. You was due last week, Wheeler.'

'Got delayed.'

'Obviously! Well, no harm done.' The agent stepped forward and took hold of Chato roughly by the arm. When the boy angrily tried to pull away, Maddocks slapped him viciously across the face with the back of his hand.

Wheeler saw red. He put a hand on the Indian agent's shoulder and spun him around to face him. 'How about trying someone your own size?' he suggested, hammering his fist into the agent's pot belly. Maddocks grunted as he sank to his knees holding his stomach. Wheeler locked eyes with the bemused-looking captain. 'No wonder the Apaches don't trust us when men like him run the agencies,' he snapped, wondering which side of the fence the army man would hang his hat.

'You had no call to do that, Wheeler,' snorted the officer, ending Wheeler's hopes of finding understanding and support for his actions.

Wheeler sighed and shook his head sadly. 'Which village is the boy assigned to?' he asked over his shoulder, as he and Chato returned to their horses.

'Most of Porico's band are camping with some Chiricahuas just south of here.'

Wheeler nodded. 'I'll take him there.' With that he and his young charge set off in the direction of the Chiricahua camp.

Late the following afternoon he entered the compound at Fort Dobbs. Folks paid him scant heed as he cantered up to the sutler's store. A familiar face greeted him when he strode in through the door in search of a cold beer to cut the dust from his dry throat. 'I'd about given up on you, pard,' said Jake Parkes with a broad grin. 'Let me buy you a drink.' He nodded towards Jock McDonald. 'I don't suppose you've heard the news?' asked Parkes, as McDonald put two beers on the bar in front of them. Wheeler frowned. 'Atkinson's got his name in the eastern newspapers. They're makin' him out to be a real old-fashioned hero too.'

'The hell you say!'

'Rumour has it he'll win hisself a medal and a big fat promotion into the bargain.'

'Someone ought to tell them newspaper folk what really happened at the Gila River.'

'They don't want the truth, laddie,' interjected McDonald from the bar. 'They want a good story and a dashing new hero for their readers.'

'Then I'm glad my scouting days are over,' said Wheeler. 'I've had about a gutful of this man's army!'

'What are you planning to do?' asked McDonald, leaning his hairy arms on the bar.

'Figured on trying my hand at a little prospecting down Tucson way. What about you, Jake?' he asked, lifting his eyes to his friend's face.

'I'm gonna head over to Fort Concho to see if they have need of another scout,' he replied. 'Why don't you ride with me, Ty? You ain't no prospector.'

Wheeler swallowed what was left of his beer and set his empty glass on the table. 'No thanks,' he replied, coming to his feet to shake hands with his friend.

'Watch your top-knot,' said Parkes, as Wheeler disappeared through the door.

Wheeler left the fort without a tinge of regret or as much as a backward glance. He turned south-east towards the mining community of Tucson, hoping to find a little silver to line his pockets and some peace of mind. As far as he was concerned his scouting days were over, but the army hadn't finished with Ty Wheeler, not by a long way.

Postscript

A high-pitched screech caused General Miles and his edgy troopers to look up towards the steep cliffs which towered over their campsite. A few of the men grabbed their rifles as they scanned the rocks for any sign of danger. But when Wheeler caught sight of an eagle gracefully winging its way to its nest high above the ground, he motioned to the general and the troopers to relax. They instantly set aside their weapons and went back to their coffee and private thoughts.

A strange silence had descended upon the camp a half-hour earlier when Lieutenant Gatewood and his two trusted Apache scouts left to parley with Geronimo. The old war chief was known to be holed up in a sheltered ravine a mile ahead. Since their departure, the atmosphere had remained very tense. Each minute which passed without word from the peace envoys only served to add to the tension.

The general emptied the luke-warm dregs from his tin cup with a flick of his wrist and refilled it from the enamel pot simmering over the fire in the centre of the camp. He nodded at Wheeler and the arrogant Tom Horn in turn. He had great respect for the older man, indeed he had played a major part in persuading him out of retirement when the top brass in Washington had given him the thankless task of bringing Geronimo to heel. However, he had little time for the sulky, self-opinionated Horn, even if he was Al Sieber's protégé. He set his cup down on a large rock and began to pace up and down impatiently, seemingly oblivious to the sultry heat of the early morning. His mind wandered back to the family and friends he hadn't seen in months. The campaign had kept him in the field even longer than he had anticipated, but with luck Gatewood would bring him good news within the hour.

The scuffling of army boots running across the rocky ground brought him out of his reverie. He heard one of the pickets shout that riders were approaching the camp. A moment later he saw Gatewood and the Apache scouts enter the draw. There was no way he could tell from their faces whether their mission had met with success or failure. Fearing the worst, he walked slowly forward to greet them.

'How about a cup of that stuff you call coffee, trooper?' suggested Gatewood to a skittish-looking young recruit, as he dismounted by the camp-fire. The soldier immediately reached for the pot, his fumble-fingered antics drawing laughter from the other troopers.

'Welcome back, Lieutenant,' said the

General. 'How'd you make out?'

'We did good,' replied Gatewood.

'You actually spoke with Geronimo himself?'

'We did,' replied Gatewood.

'And he's willing to talk terms?' asked Tom Horn. The lieutenant merely nodded.

'Can he be trusted?' asked Miles.

'I think so,' replied Gatewood casually.

'What makes you so sure?'

'His followers are half starved, General,' advised the lieutenant. 'They're also short on ammunition.'

'Yeah, but he's a wily ole fox,' argued Miles. 'What do you think, Wheeler? Does he really want to talk peace?'

Wheeler looked him straight in the eye and said, 'I don't reckon he's of a mind to fight. He's had enough of being hounded from one rocky hole to another. He'll talk.'

General Miles nodded happily, his eyes fairly twinkling with excitement. 'So be it,' he said. 'Gentlemen, let's go meet with Mr Geronimo. To us falls the honour of finally bringing an end to the Apache wars.'

★ ★ ★

The sad, plaintive whistle of the waiting locomotive and a sudden rush of steam alerted the onlookers to the imminent departure of the train. Some of the excited children gathered in the depot pushed their way through to the front of the crowd, hoping to obtain one last glimpse of stone-faced Apaches as they were herded aboard the cramped cattle trucks. The sullen Indians seemed to be lost in their own thoughts as the soldiers escorting the train began to slam the doors shut, plunging them into semi-darkness.

Deemed prisoners of war, they were bound for a living hell in the swampy, disease-ridden backwaters of Florida, hundreds of miles from their traditional hunting grounds. Most of them suspected they would never see their homeland again.

Ty Wheeler was there to see them off. It marked the end of an era. The once noble and feared Apaches no longer held dominion over the land they had called their own for centuries. Part of him felt sorry for them, even though he knew the territory would benefit from the security their defeat had brought. Arizona would prosper and grow. It would become a fit place for a man to raise a family. But it still seemed a shame that there would be no place for the Apache in the new order of things.

As he waited patiently for the train to leave, he caught sight of Geronimo sitting forlornly by a window in the one passenger car that had been provided for the Apaches' journey into exile. The two old adversaries locked eyes. Geronimo raised the chains of incarceration that bound his wrists and jingled them to show Wheeler how he was being treated. He then sagged back down on to his bench-seat, a look of abject misery on his tired, wrinkled face. The scout felt nothing but pity for his former enemy, even though he knew that the old chief had brought the punishment on himself. They were kindred spirits. Both mourned the passing of the old days and the old ways, though for very different reasons: Geronimo grieved for the passing of a way of life, the loss of his freedom and the excitement of war; Wheeler, because his life had lost some if not most of its purpose. For more than a quarter of a century he had tracked and fought the Apaches. Now it was finally over.

Neither of them fully understood the changes that were taking place in the world, even though most people viewed it as progress. They were still looking at each other when the train pulled out of the depot.

As Wheeler turned to leave he felt a sharp tug on the sleeve of his buckskin jacket. He swung around to find himself staring into a bearded face from his past. 'I just knowed you'd be here,' chortled Jake Parkes, beaming brightly.

'Jake Parkes!' exclaimed Wheeler, his own face breaking out in a broad grin. 'Well I'll be darned! What brings you here?'

'Same as you,' replied Parkes, shaking hands vigorously with his friend. 'I just wanted to see ol' Geronimo on his way.' Both of them regretted the passing of the old days and the old ways. Geronimo had been their last link with a way of life they had enjoyed for as long as they could remember, and, if truth be told, both still yearned for. 'Makes me feel kinda sad though, seeing what they've done to him. He looks mighty old now.'

Wheeler grinned. 'We all git old, my friend,' he chortled. 'I mean, just look at you, all grey hair and pot belly!'

'Looks to me like you got me beat if'n we're counting grey hairs, pard,' retorted Parkes, with a grin. 'I suppose you heard about Atkinson?' he added, changing the subject.

The very mention of the man's name caused the hairs on the back of Wheeler's neck to stand on end. 'What's that devious son-of-a-bitch bin up to now?' he demanded.

'Well I only heard the story second-hand,' said Parkes, 'but it seems the major was forced to resign his commission.'

'You ain't serious?' Parkes just grinned. 'Did you hear tell why?'

'Somit about conduct unbecoming of an officer and a gentleman.'

'What in tarnation's that supposed ta mean?'

There was a wicked glint in his friend's eye as he spoke. 'I heard that he was caught in a compromising position with some new young recruit.'

'You're kidding? The major an ol' squaw boots, well, don't that beat all?'

'Thought it might make your day.'

Wheeler chuckled and then slapped his old friend on the shoulder. 'I reckon there must be a God in heaven after all. I never reckoned on seein' that peckerless bag of hot air take a fall, but he sure as hell has, ain't he?'

'Yup,' agreed Parkes, with a huge grin. 'He sure has. Now, how about a drink for old times' sake? I'm a'buyin'.'

'Lead the way, friend,' agreed Wheeler, happily. 'I could sure do with cutting the tar from my throat.' The two of them left the depot and strolled up the dusty street towards the Red Garter saloon, reminiscing about the past and discussing future plans.

Several miles away to the east, a stone-faced, broken-hearted Geronimo sat listening to the monotonous clickety-clack of the wheels on the iron rails, contemplating the loss of the freedom he had once enjoyed. Despite the white-eyes' promise that he would be allowed to return within two years, he knew that he would never again walk the mountains and high plains that he loved. His people had fought well, but the gods had abandoned them. They had decreed that the whites should win. He closed his eyes and tried to imagine what life would be like in that far-off place called Florida. He also wondered if people would remember him in the years to come. There was no way he could have known then that the name of Geronimo would live on for ever. It is said that even today his name is carried on the wind that blows free across the plains. Like the Apache, and those who fought them, his legend will never die.

Other titles in the Linford Western Library

THE CROOKED SHERIFF
John Dyson

Black Pete Bowen quit Texas with a burning hatred of men who try to take the law into their own hands. But he discovers that things aren't much different in the silver mountains of Arizona.

THEY'LL HANG BILLY FOR SURE:
Larry & Stretch
Marshall Grover

Billy Reese, the West's most notorious desperado, was to stand trial. From all compass points came the curious and the greedy, the riff-raff of the frontier. Suddenly, a crazed killer was on the loose — but the Texas Trouble-Shooters were there, girding their loins for action.

RIDERS OF RIFLE RANGE
Wade Hamilton

Veterinarian Jeff Jones did not like open warfare — but it was there on Scrub Pine grass. When he diagnosed a sick bull on the Endicott ranch as having the contagious blackleg disease, he got involved in the warfare — whether he liked it or not!

BEAR PAW
Nevada Carter

Austin Dailey traded two cows to a pair of Indians for a bay horse, which subsequently disappeared. Tracks led to a secret hideout of fugitive Indians — and cattle thieves. Indians and stockmen co-operated against the rustlers. But it was Pale Woman who acted as interpreter between her people and the rangemen.

THE WEST WITCH
Lance Howard

Detective Quinton Hilcrest journeys west, seeking the Black Hood Bandits' lost fortune. Within hours of arriving in Hags Bend, he is fighting for his life, ensnared with a beautiful outcast the town claims is a witch! Can he save the young woman from the angry mob?

GUNS OF THE PONY EXPRESS
T. M. Dolan

Rich Zennor joined the Pony Express venture at the start, as second-in-command to tough Denning Hartman. But Zennor had the problems of Hartman believing that they had crossed trails in the past, and the fact that he was strongly attached to Hartman's Indian girl, Conchita.

BLACK JO OF THE PECOS
Jeff Blaine

Nobody knew where Black Josephine Callard came from or whither she returned. Deputy U.S. Marshal Frank Haggard would have to exercise all his cunning and ability to stay alive before he could defeat her highly successful gang and solve the mystery.

RIDE FOR YOUR LIFE
Johnny Mack Bride

They rode west, hoping for a new start. Then they met another broken-down casualty of war, and he had a plan that might deliver them from despair. But the only men who would attempt it would be the truly brave — or the desperate. They were both.

THE NIGHTHAWK
Charles Burnham

While John Baxter sat looking at the ruin that arsonists had made of his log house, a stranger rode into the yard. Baxter and Walt Showalter partnered up and re-built the house. But when it was dynamited, they struck back — and all hell broke loose.

MAVERICK PREACHER
M. Duggan

Clay Purnell was hopeful that his posting to Capra would be peaceable enough. However, on his very first day in town he rode into trouble. Although loath to use his .45, Clay found he had little choice — and his likeness to a notorious bank robber didn't help either!

SIXGUN SHOWDOWN
Art Flynn

After years as a lawman elsewhere, Dan Herrick returned to his old Arizona stamping ground to find that nesters were being driven from their homesteads by ruthless ranchers. Before putting away his gun once and for all, Dan forced a bloody and decisive showdown.

RIDE LIKE THE DEVIL!
Sam Gort

Ben Trunch arrived back on the Big T only to find that land-grabbing was in progress. He confronted Luke Fletcher, saloon-keeper and town boss, with what was happening, and was immediately forced to ride for his life. But he got the chance to put it all right in the end.

SLOW WOLF AND DAN FOX:
Larry & Stretch
Marshall Grover

The deck was stacked against an innocent man. Larry Valentine played detective, and his investigation propelled the Texas Trouble-Shooters into a gun-blazing fight to the finish.

BRANAGAN'S LAW
Alan Irwin

To Angus Flint, the valley was his domain and he didn't want any new settlers. But Texas Ranger Jim Branagan had other ideas. Could he put an end to Flint's tyranny for good?

THE DEVIL RODE A PINTO
Bret Rey

When a settler is cut to ribbons in a frenzied attack, Texas Ranger Sam Buck learns that the killer is Rufus Berry, known as The Devil. Sam stiffens his resolve to kill or capture Berry and break up his gang.

THE DEATH MAN
Lee F. Gregson
The hardest of men went in fear of Ford, the bounty hunter, who had earned the name 'The Death Man'. Yet even Ford was not infallible — when he killed the wrong man, he found that he was being sought himself by the feared Frank Ambler.

LEAD LANGUAGE
Gene Tuttle
After Blaze Colton and Ricky Rawlings have delivered a train load of cows from Arizona to San Francisco, they become involved in a load of trouble and find themselves on the run!

A DOLLAR FROM THE STAGE
Bill Morrison
Young saddle-tramp Len Finch stumbled into a web of murder, lawlessness, intrigue and evil ambition. In the end, he put his life on the line for the folks that he cared about.

BRAND 2: HARDCASE
Neil Hunter

When Ben Wyatt and his gang hold up the bank in Adobe, Wyatt is captured. Judge Rice asks Jason Brand, an ex-U.S. Marshal, to take up the silver star. Wyatt is in the cells, his men close by, and Brand is the only man to get Adobe out of real trouble . . .

THE GUNMAN AND THE ACTRESS
Chap O'Keefe

To be paid a heap of money just for protecting a fancy French actress and her troupe of players didn't seem that difficult — but Joshua Dillard hadn't banked on the charms of the actress, and the fact that someone didn't want him even to reach the town . . .

HE RODE WITH QUANTRILL
Terry Murphy

Following the break-up of Quantrill's Raiders, both Jesse James and Mel Becher head their own gang. A decade later, their paths cross again when, unknowingly, they plan to rob the same bank — leading to a violent confrontation between Becher and James.

THE CLOVERLEAF CATTLE COMPANY
Lauran Paine

Bessie Thomas believed in miracles, and her husband, Jawn Henry, did not. But after finding a murdered settler and his woman, and running down the renegades responsible, Jawn Henry would have time to reflect. He and Bessie had never had children. Miracles evidently did happen.

ing
ved
as
ap
ve
ras
ed
fe.

J
t
h
re
le
b
re
si
th